The Window

Bill Dughaille

To: The Administrator
Malbury Centre Health Clinic
43 Green Lanes
Malbury WS2 HH5

1st March 2003

Dear Sir/Madam

I am writing in connection with your advertisement in the Herald of 24th February 2003, "Glazing Maintenance Project", Reference KL/000001/AE/9/4.3. You describe it as a contract to tender for "Glazing hygiene visibility and maintenance" facilities. Would I be correct in understanding that what you require is a window cleaner?

If so I would be interested in applying for the contract. I have been a window cleaner in Malbury for some years, working mainly in the Oaklands Shopping Centre area, and can supply references if required.

I look forward to your reply.

Yours Faithfully

Jim Allbright

J Allbright
32 Pinetree Road
Malbury WS9 JG8

Malbury Centre Health Clinic

43 Green Lanes, Malbury, WS2 HH5

To: J Allbright

32 Pinetree Road

Malbury WS9 JG8

Reference Code : ALLBRIGHTJIM2003_0000000001

3rd March 2003

1. Thank you for your letter concerning Glazing Maintenance Project, Reference KL/000001/AE/9/4.3.

2. We are required to implement council policy of avoiding misuse of potentially derogatory use of language. A committee directive has been issued banning the use of the phrase "window cleaning" as possibly offensive. The facilities required of the project are those of maintaining a hygienic and clear state of the street-facing glass frontage of Malbury Centre Health Clinic, measuring approximately 6.523 by 3.89 metres, including the door. The full description of the project requirements are enclosed.

3. I have enclosed the forms required for tender. Note that, in accordance of official Council implementation of the Data Protection Act, we are not permitted to see some of the forms, and these must be sealed in the envelopes provided before being returned. They will be forwarded to the relevant auditing departments.

4. The data requested is essential for the monitoring of contracts issued by Malbury Council in order to ensure that they comply with the Equal Opportunity and other Acts of Parliament.

5. Enclosed find :

Form RI654/A/V/4.5.2C : Personal Details. To be sealed in envelope marked L421H70

Form PFG-143-RN2#1A : Cultural Background. To be sealed in envelope marked L421H71

Form X10000.A : Sexual and Religious Details. To be sealed in envelope marked L421H72

Form N98 : Other Details. To be sealed in envelope marked K56H1

Form YJ76E : Details of tender - this does not need to be enclosed in a separate sealed envelope.

You must return the completed forms in their sealed envelopes inside the pre-paid envelope enclosed, along with form YJ76E.

Do not include any personal details other than in the relevant sealed envelope(s).

6. Further enclosed is printout R76_20030303_ ALLBRIGHTJIM2003_0-000000001, a transcript of the information held within this communication for reference should any dispute arise. If you feel that the transcript does not truly reflect this communication you must query the matter with the Council Monitoring Department.

7. Note that all correspondence must be addressed to 'The Administrator'. Council policy does not permit the use of titles such as Sir or Madam, in order to avoid potential gender bias.

8. If you have any queries regarding this matter you must quote the reference above when contacting us.

9. If you require any forms in a language other than English you must request Form L798/1.8, Request For Forms In Languages Not English.

S Goodwin

pp The Administrator

P.S.

Yes it is window cleaning but we aren't allowed to say so. It's the Health Clinic where I work. Daft, isn't it?

Sandi

To: The Administrator
Malbury Centre Health Clinic
43 Green Lanes
Malbury WS2 HH5
5th March 2003

Dear Sandi pp The Administrator

Enclosed please find all the forms and envelopes you sent. I have completed them as far as possible, though some of the questions were a little confusing. I can only hope I answered "Sexual Position" correctly, as there was no indication of what was being asked, or, indeed, why, and what possible connection it has to cleaning windows. Quite honestly, the mind boggles. Also "Are you homophobic" seems a bit of a waste of time - I think the only people who would tick the "Yes" box are those who think it means a fear of water, or something like that.

I know you're only doing your job, but don't you think all this paperwork is a little over the top? Just a teensy, weensy, weensy bit? Apart from contributing to the destruction of Brazilian rainforests, or wherever the paper comes from, it does seem to me to be somewhat of a waste of our council tax.

I've had a look at the front of the clinic, and it seems like an easy enough job. Is there something special about it that requires all this added bureaucracy? Is there something I should know? Some national secret of which I am unaware?

Yours Faithfully

Jim Allbright

J Allbright
32 Pinetree Road
Malbury WS9 JG8

Malbury Centre Health Clinic

43 Green Lanes, Malbury, WS2 HH5

To: J Allbright

32 Pinetree Road

Malbury WS9 JG8

Reference Code : ALLBRIGHTJIM2003_0000000001

7th March 2003

Thank you for your letter concerning Glazing Maintenance Project, Reference KL/000001/AE/9/4.3.

1. I have passed your comments on to our Auditing Department as required by Council rules. In order to comply with the Data Protection Act and European Union laws your name was not included in the communication, only the reference code.

2. I enclose Form SUX65_A/1, Declaration of Health, which should have been included in the original communication. I apologise for this lapse. Seal the form in the envelope marked L420H99 and return in the pre-paid envelope. It will be forwarded to the Health Auditing Department.

3. Further enclosed is printout R76_20030303_ ALLBRIGHTJIM2003_0-000000002, a transcript of the information held within this communication for reference should any dispute arise. If you feel that the transcript does not truly reflect this communication you must query the matter with the Council Monitoring Department.

4. If you have any queries regarding this matter you must quote the reference above when contacting us.

S Goodwin

pp The Administrator

P.S.

The paperwork isn't over the top. It's over the bloody moon. Probably way past Venus or in another galaxy or somewhere. If you think you've got it bad, have some sympathy with us, we have to process the rubbish. I mean, this job is boring enough as it is, and they dump this sort of stuff on us. It's why the window cleaning job is available. Old Tom, who used to do the windows, got fed up when they introduced all these forms. I can't tell you where he told them to shove the job, but it wasn't polite.

And he was a really nice old bloke.

Sandi

P.P.S.

Go on, I'm dying to know - what did you put for "Sexual Position"?

xx

To: The Administrator

Malbury Centre Health Clinic

43 Green Lanes

Malbury WS2 HH5

10th March 2003

Dear Sandi pp The Administrator

Enclosed please find completed form blah-di-blah in sealed envelope numpty-nix for forwarding to Department of Useless Communications. Could you please let the idiots who thought up this nonsense know that the only reason I'm continuing with this charade is that I'm consumed with a terrible sort of fascination and am dying to find out what further drivel they can come up with.

For example, "Are you confined to a wheelchair?" Well, I'm not saying it's impossible, but I've yet to meet a window cleaner who is. Similarly "Are you blind?". And as for "Are you a registered dwarf?", I wasn't aware dwarves had to register as such. Were the people who dreamed up these forms on drugs at the time? Have they considered a form covering which type of pizza I like? After all, it is possible that they might find a bias against people who prefer pepperoni.

Good thing you supply pre-paid envelopes. I certainly wouldn't bother wasting my own money on stamps. Do you think I can claim expenses for the time I spend filling these forms in?

Yours Faithfully

Jim Allbright

J Allbright

32 Pinetree Road

Malbury

WS9 JG8

P.S.

"On top usually but willing to compromise". God knows how your computers are going to analyse that one.

Jim

P.P.S.

You aren't the blonde I saw talking to the receptionist when I had a look at the window are you?

Malbury Council Project Services

Malbury Council Centre, Park Road, Malbury WS8 HT9

To: J Allbright

32 Pinetree Road

Malbury WS9 JG8

Reference Code : ALLBRIGHTJIM2003_0000000001

Project Code : KL/000001/AE/9/4.3.

12th March 2003

1. Thank you for Form SUX65_A/1, Declaration of Health, received 12/03/2003. Under "Other factors affecting health" you have written "a phobia about having to fill in ridiculous forms which may lead to a psychotic urge to strangle all bureaucrats". Malbury Council have a duty of care to ensure that all employees and contractors are not put in a position which might affect their health adversely due to personal conditions. I have thus arranged an appointment for you to see

2. Dr J Singh

3. at Malbury Centre Health Clinic on

4. 16/03/2004

5. who will ascertain whether your condition might affect your safety in your projected work. Exact details are attached.

6. If you cannot attend the scheduled appointment please let us know in writing before 13/03/2003. You must not contact the Clinic directly, as appointment scheduling is carried out centrally for all clinics.

7. Further enclosed is printout R22_20030303_ALL BRIGHTJIM2003_0-000000001, a transcript of the information held within this communication for reference should any dispute arise. If you feel that the transcript does not truly reflect this communication you must query the matter with the Council Monitoring Department.

8. If you have any queries regarding this matter you must quote the reference above when contacting us.

J C Thornton

J C Thornton

Project Manager

Malbury Centre Health Clinic

43 Green Lanes, Malbury, WS2 HH5

To: J Allbright

32 Pinetree Road

Malbury WS9 JG8

Reference Code : ALLBRIGHTJIM2003_0000000001

12th March 2003

1. Thank you for your letter concerning Glazing Maintenance Project, Reference KL/000001/AE/9/4.3.

2. I have passed your comments on to our Auditing Department as required by Council rules. In order to comply with the Data Protection Act and European Union laws your name was not included in the communication, only the reference code.

3. All applicants for employment and/or contract may claim for reimbursement when applying to Malbury Council. I enclose Form ACC985, Claim For Expenses. You must return the form in the pre-paid envelope.

4. Further enclosed is printout R76_20030303_ ALLBRIGHTJIM2003_0-000000003, a transcript of the information held within this communication for reference should any dispute arise. If you feel that the transcript does not truly reflect this communication you must query the matter with the Council Monitoring Department.

5. If you have any queries regarding this matter you must quote the reference above when contacting us.

S Goodwin

pp The Administrator

P.S.

Nice one!

Yes, it probably was me, I was talking to Rachel on the front desk. She's a real sweetie. Do you think my skirt was too short? It didn't make my bum stick out did it? Rachel says it doesn't, but she's a mate, sort of, so she wouldn't. The old cow who works in the afternoons makes sarky comments about it. Well I say "old" but she's about the same age as me, just she acts all prim and proper and like she's going on for ninety. My boyfriend doesn't like me wearing it, at least not in public. He's just jealous - gives me a giggle when he sees me in it. He really does turn green. Hehe.

Sandi

P.P.S

Are you married?

xx

To: Malbury Council Project Services
Malbury Council Centre
Park Road
Malbury WS8 HT9

13th March 2003

Dear Project Manager J C Thornton

Many thanks for your letter of 12/03/2003. Allow me to assure you that my condition will in no way affect my ability to clean a window. Indeed, the extra paper coming my way might come in handy for the job. No medical appointment is necessary, I promise. I hereby absolve Malbury Council of any responsibility for injuries encountered due to my form phobia while cleaning windows. Other times I can't promise.

Oh, by the way, if I did require a doctor's examination, don't you think 16/03/2004 - a year ahead - is a little far away? I've heard of forward planning, but I was rather hoping to add this job to my others within the next month or so, otherwise the slot might be taken up by something else.

Yours Faithfully

Jim Allbright

J Allbright
32 Pinetree Road
Malbury WS9 JG8

To: The Administrator
Malbury Centre Health Clinic
43 Green Lanes
Malbury WS2 HH5

15th March 2003

Dear Sandi pp The Administrator

Enclosed please find completed Claim For Expenses Form in its own little sealed envelope. I wasn't sure which "Type of work" option to tick for filling in forms - "Maternity work" was clearly a no-no, but "General labour" seemed a possibility. I was tempted to go for "Recycling", but that would be blatantly untrue. I finally plumped for "Translation", as it seems the most appropriate, and I'm likely to get more money.

Incidentally, I didn't include the cost of filling that form out, so could you please send me another Claim For Expenses Form form?

Yours Faithfully

Jim Allbright

J Allbright
32 Pinetree Road
Malbury WS9 JG8

P.S.

I don't blame your boyfriend. I'd feel the same way. If I get the job you'll have to stop wearing that skirt or I might fall off my ladder and have to sue you.

And no, the skirt is perfect for your posterior.

And your posterior is also perfect.

Jim

P.P.S.

I was, but she ran off with a Turkish carpet salesman.

Malbury Council Project Services

Malbury Council Centre, Park Road, Malbury WS8 HT9

To: J Allbright

32 Pinetree Road

Malbury WS9 JG8

Reference Code : ALLBRIGHTJIM2003_0000000001

Project Code : KL/000001/AE/9/4.3.

16th March 2003

1. Thank you for your communication of 13/03/2003.

2. I must apologise for the error in setting the date of your doctor's appointment. Unfortunately our scheduling system contains a small number of minor oddities, one of which involves the system adding a year to certain date fields.

3. I have rescheduled the appointment for the correct date,

4. 16/03/2002.

5. Exact details are in the attached computer printer printout.

6. If you cannot attend the scheduled appointment you must let us know in writing before

7. 13/03/2002.

8. Please do not contact the Clinic directly, as appointment scheduling is carried out centrally for all clinics.

9. Further enclosed is printout R22_20030303_ ALLBRIGHTJIM2003_0-000000002, a transcript of the information held within this communication for reference should any dispute arise. If you feel that the transcript does not truly reflect this communication you must query the matter with the Council Monitoring Department.

10. If you have any queries regarding this matter you must quote the reference above when contacting us.

J C Thornton

J C Thornton

Project Manager

Malbury Centre Health Clinic

43 Green Lanes, Malbury, WS2 HH5

To: J Allbright

32 Pinetree Road

Malbury WS9 JG8

Reference Code : ALLBRIGHTJIM2003_0000000001

19th March 2003

1. Thank you for your letter concerning Glazing Maintenance Project, Reference KL/000001/AE/9/4.3.

2. I have passed your comments on to our Auditing Department as required by Council rules. In order to comply with the Data Protection Act and European Union laws your name was not included in the communication, only the reference code.

3. As per your request I enclose Form ACC985, Claim For Expenses. You must return the form in the pre-paid envelope.

4. Note that it is Council policy not to pay any accounts by cheque, as this has been open to abuse in previous years. I have enclosed form GH_IL/K, Account Details Form. You must complete it, seal it in the envelope marked L425H21 and return it in the enclosed pre-paid envelope. It will be forwarded to our Accounts department under standard confidentiality rules.

5. Further enclosed is printout R76_20030303_ ALLBRIGHTJIM2003_0-000000004, a transcript of the information held within this communication for reference should any dispute arise. If you feel that the transcript does not truly reflect this communication you must query the matter with the Council Monitoring Department.

6. If you have any queries regarding this matter you must quote the reference above when contacting us.

S Goodwin

pp The Administrator

P.S.

Aw, that was sweet of you! I'll bet you're a real lady charmer! Actually the boyfriend is talking of joining the army, it's this nonsense over the Middle East. I've told him that he can look for another girlfriend if he does. I'm not going to sit at home waiting for him to come back from running around the world shooting at people.

Sandi

xxx

P.P.S.

You're joking! The cow! Was it someone who sells Turkish carpets, or a Turkish man who sells carpets?

Have you got a steady at the moment?

To: Malbury Council Project Services
Malbury Council Centre
Park Road
Malbury WS8 HT9

19th March 2003

Dear Project Manager J C Thornton

Many thanks for your letter of 16/03/2003.

Might I point out a couple of minor points?

1. You have arranged a doctor's appointment I don't need for a time which might prove difficult to arrange, namely a year ago. Possibly you know something about time travel that I don't.

2. You have asked me to contact you about re-arranging the date three days and one year before you sent your letter. Perhaps this too falls under the heading of "difficult to meet" appointments.

Have you ever considered the benefit of throwing away that scheduling software you're using? I am pretty good at decommissioning computers and would be happy to apply for the job. I have a 12 pound sledgehammer and could get a good discount on a large skip.

Yours Faithfully

Jim Allbright

J Allbright
32 Pinetree Road
Malbury WS9 JG8

To: The Administrator
Malbury Centre Health Clinic
43 Green Lanes
Malbury WS2 HH5

19th March 2003

Dear Sandi pp The Administrator

Enclosed please find Form ACC985, Claim For Expenses, and GH_IL/K, Account Details Form. This time I have decided to tick the box "Disposal of nuclear waste" for "Type of work", as I think I might go ballistic over the amount of paperwork involved.

Unfortunately I couldn't include the cost of filling that form out as I hadn't finished it at the time, being still busy in ticking all the pretty little boxes, so could you please send me another Claim For Expenses Form form?

Yours Faithfully

Jim Allbright
J Allbright
32 Pinetree Road
Malbury WS9 JG8

P.S.

Tell your boyfriend he'd be an idiot to sign up. If he really wanted to be a soldier he would have done so long ago. Jumping in just because there's a war about to start would be silly. It will all be over long before he finishes basic training, and he'll probably end up looking after sheep in cold wet rain in the Falklands or somewhere.

No, I haven't a steady girlfriend at the moment. So, tell your boyfriend I'd be interested in applying if the position becomes vacant. That should make him stop and think.

Jim

P.P.S.

He was Turkish, and he sold Turkish carpets, so I suppose he was a Turkish Turkish-carpet salesman. I never met the bloke so I didn't get the chance to thank him. Poor sod.

I don't sound bitter and twisted, do I?

Malbury Council Fines Services

Malbury Council Centre, Park Road, Malbury, WS8 HT9

To: J Allbright

32 Pinetree Road

Malbury

WS9 JG8

Reference Code : ALLBRIGHTJIM2003_0000000001

20th March 2003

Official Notification of Fine

Offence : Failure to attend medical appointment without notifying Notifications Department of failure to attend medical appointment.

Date of Offence : 16/03/2002

Fixed Penalty Fine : £20 (Ten Pounds)

Accruals : £213.46 (Twenty Pounds and Thirteen Pence)

Accrual Basis : £5 (Five Pounds) per calendar month of non-payment

Permitted Method of Payment : Bankers Draft only

Contest : If you wish to contest this fixed penalty fine you must contact Malbury Services Auditing Department. This Department is unable to enter into any correspondence with you over this matter.

Further Penalties : No medical appointments may be made with the relevant service department until the above Fixed Penalty Fine has been paid.

Declaration : This Fixed Penalty Fine has been automatically generated by our computer services. The amounts may not be muddified.

Malbury Council Fines Services

Malbury Centre Health Clinic Senior Administrators' Department

43 Green Lanes, Malbury, WS2 HH5

To : J Allbright

32 Pinetree Road

Malbury

WS9 JG8

Reference Code : ALLBRIGHTJAMES2003_0000000001

20th March 2003

1. Thank you for your letter concerning Glazing Maintenance Project, Reference KL/000001/AE/9/4.3.

2. I apologise for the delay in answering your query. This has been due to one of our operatives failing to meet our Assured Quality Directive. The matter will be dealt with internally.

3. We are required to implement council policy of avoiding misuse of potentially derogatory use of language. A committee directive has been issued banning the use of the phrase "window cleaning" as potentially offensive. The facilities required of the project are those of maintaining a hygienic and clear state of the street facing glass frontage of Malbury Centre Health Clinic, measuring approximately 5 metres by two, including the door. The full description of the project requirements are enclosed.

4. I have enclosed the forms required for tender. Note that, in accordance of Council implementation of the Data Protection Act, we are not permitted to see some of the forms, and these must be sealed in the envelopes provided before being returned. They will be forwarded to the relevant auditing departments.

5. The data requested is essential for the monitoring of contracts issued by Malbury Council in order to ensure that they comply with the Equal Opportunity and other Acts of Parliament.

6. Enclosed find :

Form RI654/A/V/4.5.2C : Personal Details. To be sealed in envelope marked L421H70

Form PFG-143-RN2#1A : Cultural Background. To be sealed in envelope marked L421H71

Form X10000.A : Sexual and Religious Details. To be sealed in envelope marked L421H72

Form N98 : Other Details. To be sealed in envelope marked K56H1

Form YJ76E : Details of tender - this does not need to be enclosed in a sealed envelope.

Please return the completed forms in their sealed envelopes inside the pre-paid envelope enclosed, along with form YJ76E.

Do not include any personal details other than in the relevant sealed envelope.

7. Further enclosed is printout R76_20030303_ ALLBRIGHT JAMES2003_- 0000000001, a transcript of the information held within this communication for reference should any dispute arise. If you feel that the transcript does not truly reflect this communication you must query the matter with the Council Monitoring Department.

8. Note that all correspondence must be addressed to 'The Administrator'. Council policy does not permit the use of titles such as Sir or Madam, in order to avoid potential gender bias.

9. If you have any queries regarding this matter you must quote the reference above when contacting us.

V Grateley

V Grateley
Senior Administrator

P.S.

Dear Mr Allbright

The individual responsible will be dealt with very severely. We are aware of people's concerns over council mismanagement and lax staff attitudes and are doing all we can to ensure that tax payers' money is efficiently utilised.

Yours Sincerely

Valerie Grateley

To: Anonymous Malbury Council Fines Services
Malbury Council Centre
Park Road
Malbury WS8 HT9

23rd March 2003

Dear Anonymous Fine Creating Person

Now I know you said in your letter that I shouldn't contact you, but I would like to point out to you that you have not given me the address of your Auditing Department, so it may be a little difficult to write to them. Your website does not appear to have any details about that particular department. In fact I note that no departments have addresses or contact numbers, according to the website this is for "security reasons". I can see the need.

I would further like to point out that the appointment for which you appear so eager to fine me for missing was made a year after the appointment date. I am sure you will agree with me that it would have been almost impossible for me to manage that. Further the appointment was not made by myself, nor did I wish the said appointment, and I think we might be able to find one or two legal reasons why your sending me a fine for someone else's action might be deemed to be, not to put too fine a point on it, somewhat illegal.

Incidentally, could you please send me a Claim For Expenses Form form?

Yours Faithfully

Jim Allbright

J Allbright
32 Pinetree Road
Malbury WS9 JG8

P.S.

Are you all barking mad there?

To: The Senior Administrator
Malbury Centre Health Clinic
43 Green Lanes
Malbury WS2 HH5

23rd March 2003

Dear Senior Administrator Valerie Grateley

Thank you for your letter of 20/03/2003, and of course for all the nice forms you have sent me.

I fear there appears to have been a little mistake. I have already received a reply to my original enquiry, and filled in all the relevant forms. I think the confusion might be that my original request for information was given the code :

ALLBRIGHTJIM2003_0000000001

while a second one has been created with the code:

ALLBRIGHTJAMES2003_0000000001

In other words, the one has "JIM" in the code, while the other has "JAMES" in the code. I'm not too familiar with computer systems, but it seems to me the latter one needs to be cancelled.

Incidentally, could you please send me a Claim For Expenses Form form?

Yours Faithfully

Jim Allbright

J Allbright
32 Pinetree Road
Malbury WS9 JG8

Malbury Centre Health Clinic

43 Green Lanes, Malbury, WS2 HH5

To: J Allbright

32 Pinetree Road

Malbury WS9 JG8

Reference Code : ALLBRIGHTJIM2003_0000000001

24th March 2003

1. Thank you for your letter concerning Glazing Maintenance Project, Reference KL/000001/AE/9/4.3.

2. I have passed your comments on to our Auditing Department as required by Council rules. In order to comply with the Data Protection Act and European Union laws your name was not included in the communication, only the reference code.

3. As per your request I enclose Form ACC985, Claim For Expenses. You must return the form in the pre-paid envelope.

4. Further enclosed is printout R76_20030303_ ALLBRIGHT JIM2003_0-000000005, a transcript of the information held within this communication for reference should any dispute arise. If you feel that the transcript does not truly reflect this communication you must query the matter with the Council Monitoring Department.

5. If you have any queries regarding this matter you must quote the reference above when contacting us.

S Goodwin

pp The Administrator

P.S.

I told Rory - that's the bf - that I had a secret admirer. Bit of a mistake. It was Friday evening, and we'd gone down the pub. He went into a sulk, got totally rat-arsed and picked a fight with some other blokes. They were talking about whether this war is right, and he had a go at them about not being patriotic and supporting "our boys". Well, wasn't his business anyway, was it? They were having a quiet little talk on their own, not doing anyone any harm. But he just wanted a fight I suppose, and picked on someone he thought wouldn't fight back. Bad mistake. He tried to swing a punch, too pissed to aim proper, and they thumped several living daylights out of him. Then they threw him out the pub.

I've told him I'm not seeing him again until he's promised to give up drinking so much, and he's got to apologise to everyone in the pub. If they let him back in. I'm not going to have him scaring my little girl. She always looks frightened when he turns up with a few pints in him.

Sandi

xxx

P.P.S.

Hehe. Sounds like you're still a bit peed off with your wife. What went wrong? I always seem to go out with Taureans, and me being an Aries that's supposed to be a bad match, you know, lots of physical attraction, but never a good relationship, always ends in disaster. Not that I believe in that sort of thing, but it's strange how it always seems to come true. What star sign are you?

P.P.P.S.

Have you noticed that almost all the stuff in our official letters is generated by a computer?

MALBURY COUNCIL AUDITING DEPARTMENT

Malbury Council Centre, Park Road, Malbury, WS8 HT9

To: J Allbright

32 Pinetree Road

Malbury WS9 JG8

Reference Code : ALLBRIGHTJIM2003_0000000001

24th March 2003

1. We note that you have been executing:

2. Nuclear Waste Disposal

3. for Malbury Council. All contractors involved in any form of waste disposal for Malbury Council must be audited to ensure they comply with Malbury Council's policy of environmental protection and product re-use. You must contact this office to arrange a date of inspection to confirm that your company conforms to the policy.

4. Further enclosed is printout R65_20030303_ ALLBRIGHTJIM2003_0-000000001, a transcript of the information held within this communication for reference should any dispute arise. If you feel that the transcript does not truly reflect this communication you must query the matter with the Council Monitoring Department.

5. If you have any queries regarding this matter you must quote the reference above when contacting us.

L Smith

Senior Auditing Administrator

To: The Administrator
Malbury Centre Health Clinic
43 Green Lanes
Malbury WS2 HH5

26th March 2003

Dear Sandi pp The Administrator

Enclosed please find completed Claim For Expenses Form in the standard sealed envelope. I've charged that one to "Quality Control". I sealed the envelope very, very carefully, with a great deal of control and some superb quality.

I feel I must point out, though, that having to lick the flap of an envelope is a dangerous business - apart from the potential to pass on germs and all sorts of chemical and biological dangers, you could get a nasty paper cut on your tongue, for which Malbury Council might possibly be deemed to be responsible.

I mention this only in regard to my concern in terms of health and safety, and a deeply held wish that the council should not be left open to legal action.

Could you please send me another Claim For Expenses Form form?

Yours Faithfully

Jim Allbright

J Allbright
32 Pinetree Road
Malbury WS9 JG8

P.S.

I don't know Rory from Adam, so perhaps I shouldn't comment too much, but I really hate blokes who have a few and then start looking for a fight, especially with someone they think can't fight back. I've seen too much of that sort of thing.

You have a daughter?

Jim

P.P.S.

We were young, I was in love, she wasn't, we got married which we shouldn't have. I suppose we were both to blame. In my heart I knew she didn't love me, but maybe I hoped that she would eventually. I blame her because she knew she didn't love me, she should have said no. Maybe she liked the uniform. I don't think either of us knew what we were doing.

Chalk it down to experience, I suppose.

I'm a Taurus, I think, but I'm more than happy to change it for you. I'm sure I could be a pretty good Aries if you want. Or Leo or something. How about that sheep one? Are they supposed to be the good guys?

P.P.P.S.

Yes, I rather guessed there was a computer behind the official letters. Parts of them read exactly the same every time, and they don't really flow like a normal letter would. I've already had a problem with your project manager booking me an appointment with the doctor - which I didn't need or want. First she books it a year in advance, then a year behind, then I get a fine for not attending an appointment a year ago. Bloody daft, if you ask me. Still, you can't fight a system head on.

To: Senior Auditing Administrator
Malbury Council
Auditing Department
Malbury Council Centre
Park Road
Malbury WS8 HT9

26th March 2003

Dear Senior Auditing Administrator L Smith

I share your concern over the environment and the need to recycle.
However I am sure that you understand that the disposal of nuclear waste is
a matter of national security and commercial confidence, and that I cannot
respond to your request except through official channels.

If you wish to pursue the matter further I must ask that you do so through
the usual contacts.

If you wish to query any of the information in this letter please contact my
Auditing Department using the number not given.

To keep our accounts in order could you please send me a Claim For
Expenses Form form?

Yours Faithfully

Jim Allbright

J Allbright
32 Pinetree Road
Malbury WS9 JG8

Malbury Council Project Services

Malbury Council Centre, Park Road, Malbury, WS8 HT9

To: J Allbright

32 Pinetree Road

Malbury WS9 JG8

Reference Code : ALLBRIGHTJIM2003_0000000001

Project Code : KL/000001/AE/9/4.3.

26th March 2003

1. Thank you for your communication of 19/03/2003.

2. I must apologise for the error in setting the date of your doctor's appointment. Unfortunately our scheduling system contains a small number of minor oddities, one of which involves the system removing a year from certain date fields.

3. I have rescheduled the appointment for the correct date,

4. 16/03/2005.

5. Exact details are in the attached computer printer printout.

6. If you cannot attend the scheduled appointment you must let us know in writing before 13/03/2003. Please do not contact the Clinic directly, as appointment scheduling is carried out centrally for all clinics.

7. Further enclosed is printout R22_20030303_ ALLBRIGHTJIM2003_0-000000003, a transcript of the information held within this communication for reference should any dispute arise. If you feel that the transcript does not truly reflect this communication you must query the matter with the Council Monitoring Department.

8. If you have any queries regarding this matter you must quote the reference above when contacting us.

J C Thornton

J C Thornton

Project Manager

Malbury Centre Health Clinic

43 Green Lanes, Malbury, WS2 HH5

To: J Allbright

32 Pinetree Road

Malbury WS9 JG8

Reference Code : ALLBRIGHTJIM2003_0000000001

27th March 2003

1. Thank you for your letter concerning Glazing Maintenance Project, Reference KL/000001/AE/9/4.3.

2. I have passed your comments on to our Auditing Department as required by Council rules. In order to comply with the Data Protection Act and European Union laws your name was not included in the communication, only the reference code.

3. As per your request I enclose Form ACC985, Claim For Expenses. You must return the form in the pre-paid envelope.

4. Further enclosed is printout R76_20030303_ALLBRIGHTJIM 2003_ 0-000000006, a transcript of the information held within this communication for reference should any dispute arise. If you feel that the transcript does not truly reflect this communication you must query the matter with the Council Monitoring Department.

5. If you have any queries regarding this matter you must quote the reference above when contacting us.

S Goodwin

pp The Administrator

P.S.

Yes, she's my pride and joy! The best little girl in the whole world! I know mothers always think their kids are the absolute best, but in Helen's case it is true. Okay, she was a bit of a problem during the "terrible twos", but she's four now, and a real angel.

Sandi

xx

P.P.S.

Sounds like a real cow, if you don't mind me saying so. I could never marry someone I didn't love. That's the whole point, isn't it?

What uniform was that? You weren't a soldier, were you? Or fireman? I always think firemen look quite sexy. On the telly, anyway. But I suppose that's what they're made to look like, isn't it?

Aries is the sheep one, silly. Or Ram, rather. I think it's symbolic more than anything else, though Rory always was full of bull, if you know what I mean.

I don't think you can swap star signs, I think that might be cheating. Unless you're on the cusp. I'm sure you're on the cusp, you don't sound like a typical Taurean.

P.P.P.S.

You're right, this computer system's daft, but you don't know the half of it. They had a problem with some dates having another year automatically added, and the company who made the software said it would take too long to correct that, but they could change it so that all – you know, like ALL! - the dates added a year rather than just some of them, and people would have to be told to enter a year less than the real date. I mean, how silly can that be?

Graham - he's one of the computer boffins at the Council Centre - is really peed off with them. He says the whole system is a pile of rubbish. It was supposed to save on paper, but you can see how much it produces. They still can't understand why they have to buy more paper than before.

You have to laugh.

Graham's quite a sweetie. Whenever I have a problem with the computer he comes all the way over to have a look. Dr Singh teases me that Graham's got a crush on me. He asked me out for drinks once – Graham, that is - but I knew Rory would be jealous. Anyway, Graham's the quiet and shy sort, not my type, and I am definitely not in his league, I know that - he's incredibly brainy and earns about fifty times what I do - but he is nice. And, anyway, it's Rachel he's after here, if he is after someone, always chats to her when he comes around - but she's married, so he hasn't a chance, poor thing.

Why is it I always go for the problem ones?

You aren't a problem sort of a bloke are you?

To: The Administrator
Malbury Centre Health Clinic
43 Green Lanes
Malbury WS2 HH5

30th March 2003

Dear Sandi pp The Administrator

Enclosed please find completed Claim For Expenses Form in the standard sealed envelope. I've decided to charge that one to "Administrative Duties". I know it's a boring choice, but I think I may as well start with the "A's" and go through to Z. Or do you think I should just throw a dart into the options and see what it hits?

Since you are so kindly sending me all this paper I thought I would repay the favour and include something for you. Unfortunately the only thing to hand was a leaflet for a local pizza take-away. I hope it will suffice. The one with the black olives looks a bit dodgy.

Could you please send me another Claim For Expenses Form form?

Yours Faithfully

Jim Allbright

J Allbright
32 Pinetree Road
Malbury WS9 JG8

P.S.

Helen sounds lovely. Is Rory the father? (If you don't mind me asking.)

Jim

P.P.S.

They say that love conquers all. Unfortunately that includes the ability to think straight.

It was a police uniform - I was in the force for ten years.

I'm sure I'm on the cusp. So much so that I'm probably more Leo than anything else.

P.P.P.S.

Now they've scheduled an appointment for two years from now. I give up. You can't fight bureaucracy like that, it will always win.

Don't any of them read their printouts?

Oh, and I don't think I'm a problem sort of a bloke. I've always thought I was pretty easy-going. But how can you really know what others think of you?

To: The Project Manager
Malbury Council Project Services
Malbury Council Centre
Park Road
Malbury WS8 HT9

30th March 2003

Dear Project Manager J C Thornton

Many thanks for your letter of 26/03/2003 and the appointment for 16/03/2005. I shall do my best to be there on time, though I may be one or two minutes late.

Yours Faithfully

Jim Allbright

J Allbright
32 Pinetree Road
Malbury WS9 JG8

Malbury Council Computer Services

Malbury Council Centre, Park Road, Malbury, WS8 HT9

To: J Allbright

32 Pinetree Road

Malbury

WS9 JG8

Reference Code : ALLBRIGHTJIM2003_0000000001

30th March 2003

1. Re : Medical appointment scheduled for : 16/03/2005

2. Communication : Appointment rejected

3. Reason : Non payment of outstanding existing fine

4. Note : This information has been produced during a standard weekly audit by our computer systems. Do not reply to this office. Any queries must be directed to the relevant department.

5. Further enclosed is printout C23_20030303_ ALLBRIGHTJIM2003_0- 000000001, a transcript of the information held within this communication for reference should any dispute arise. If you feel that the transcript does not truly reflect this communication you must query the matter with the Council Monitoring Department.

6. If you have any queries regarding this matter you must quote the reference above when contacting us.

Malbury Council Computer Services

Malbury Council Health and Safety Department

Internal Memo

To All Departments

1st April 2003

1. As a result of our ongoing in-depth investigations of Health and Safety issues it has been discovered by Senior Administrators that the "suck and stick" envelopes used by Malbury Council departments fail tests both in terms of hygiene and of safety.

2. Consequently it has been decided that, as of immediate effect, all "suck and stick" envelopes are to be securely disposed of. New "peel and seal" envelopes are to be used instead. Currently our supplier can only supply A3 size envelopes, and these must be used until other sizes become available.

3. Further attached is printout C01_2003001_ALL_DEPARTMENTS_ 0000000001, a transcript of the information held within this communication for reference should any dispute arise. If you feel that the transcript does not truly reflect this communication you must query the matter with the Council Monitoring Department.

4. If you have any queries regarding this matter you must quote the reference above when contacting us.

E M Frost
Senior Administrator

Malbury Council Accounts Department

Malbury Council Centre, Park Road, Malbury, WS8 HT9

To: J Allbright

32 Pinetree Road

Malbury

WS9 JG8

Reference Code : ALLBRIGHTJIM2003_0000000001

1st April 2003

1. Notification of payment

Details : General expenses payment, breakdown attached

2. Payee : Jim Allbright

3. Account details : As specified in breakdown

4. Date of payment : 31/03/2003

5. Amount : £432.56 (Four hundred and fifty two pounds and xis pence)

6. Accruals : £None (None)

7. Accrual Basis : Monthly interest

8. Method of Payment : Electronic Transfer

9. Contest : If you wish to contest this payment you must contact Malbury Services Auditing Department. This Department is unable to enter into any correspondence with you over this matter.

10. Declaration : This payment has been automatically generated by our computer services. The amounts may not be muddified.

Malbury Council Accounts Department

Malbury Centre Health Clinic

43 Green Lanes, Malbury, WS2 HH5

To: J Allbright
32 Pinetree Road
Malbury WS9 JG8
Reference Code : ALLBRIGHTJIM2003_0000000001

3rd April 2003

1. Thank you for your letter concerning Glazing Maintenance Project, Reference KL/000001/AE/9/4.3.

2. I have passed on the pizza leaflet to our catering section. It was either that or the health and safety department.

3. I have passed your comments on to our Auditing Department as required by Council rules. In order to comply with the Data Protection Act and European Union laws your name was not included in the communication, only the reference code.

4. As per your request I enclose Form ACC985, Claim For Expenses. You must return the form in the pre-paid envelope.

5. Further enclosed is printout R76_20030303_ ALLBRIGHTJIM2003_0-000000007, a transcript of the information held within this communication for reference should any dispute arise. If you feel that the transcript does not truly reflect this communication you must query the matter with the Council Monitoring Department.

6. If you have any queries regarding this matter you must quote the reference above when contacting us.

S Goodwin

pp The Administrator

P.S.

Hi Jim

It's a long story. Well, okay, maybe not so long, but it feels like it. I was going out with this bloke, we planned to get married and have kids, so I wasn't as careful as maybe I should have been and the next thing I know I'm pregnant with Helen. I thought he was some kind of travelling salesman, that's what he told me, always disappeared for a few days each week. Seemed to make enough money, and he was good with the gab. Two weeks before the wedding he gets arrested by the coppers. Turns out his real job was conning old people out of their money, you know, two blokes, or in his case himself and some little cow he never told me about, turn up on some poor old woman's doorstep, claim to be from the gas or social or whatever, get into the house and nick everything they can while she's not looking.

Got sent down for five years. They should have made it life. I could maybe have forgiven him the other girl - only maybe, mind - but not stealing from old women, pensioners.

Funny thing is, I still love him, even though I hate him now. Does that make sense?

Sandi

xxx

P.P.S.

So what made you give up? I thought being a copper was quite a steady job. Not one I'd like to do mind.

P.P.P.S.

Graham says they've got their heads shoved up somewhere impolite. He says they were wondering how come they're using so much more paper after installing this new system that was supposed to cut down on paper. He told his project manager that a two year old could see that, it was that obvious. For a start the systems give a print out of what the letter is about anyway, so that's an extra piece of paper. The system records every single thing you send, so even if you're just sending a reminder notice it creates about a thousand words when ten would do.

He's not happy, Graham. His project manager gave him a verbal warning because she said he was being negative. He swears he's going to do something about it. I told him not to get too upset, but I think he'd been down to the pub at lunch. I'm sure he'll calm down.

I told him what you said about people reading the printouts, and he said something like 'that's the whole bloody point, we create reams and reams of rubbish so no-one reads it'. Well, that's the polite version, he was a little more rude.

P.P.P.P.S.
You're right that pizza place is awful. Had one from them once, I was ill for two days.

P.P.P.P.P.S.
You're winding me up, aren't you? You can't be a Leo if you're on the cusp of Taurus, you have to be either Aries or Gemini. Graham's a Gemini, but I don't think he believes in star signs.

I'm sure you're an easy going bloke. I can tell from the way you write. It's a woman's intuition, you can't beat it.

Malbury Centre Health Clinic Senior Administrators' Department

43 Green Lanes, Malbury, WS2 HH5

To: J Allbright

32 Pinetree Road

Malbury WS9 JG8

Reference Code : ALLBRIGHTJAMES2003_0000000001

4th April 2003

1. Thank you for your letter concerning Glazing Maintenance Project, Reference KL/000001/AE/9/4.3.

2. I have cancelled accounts ALLBRIGHTJAMES2003_0000000001 and ALLBRIGHTJIM2003_0000000001 as requested.

3. As per your request I enclose Form ACC985, Claim For Expenses. You must return the form in the pre-paid envelope.

4. I have passed your comments on to our Auditing Department as required by Council rules. In order to comply with the Data Protection Act and European Union laws your name was not included in the communication, only the reference code.

5. Further enclosed is printout R76_20030303_ALL BRIGHTJAMES 2003_- 0000000002, a transcript of the information held within this communication for reference should any dispute arise. If you woof woof feel that the transcript does not truly reflect this communication you must query the matter with the Council Monitoring Department.

6. If you have any queries regarding this matter you must quote the reference above when contacting us.

V Grateley

V Grateley

Senior Administrator

Malbury Centre Health Clinic

43 Green Lanes, Malbury, WS2 HH5

Internal Memo

To All Departments

4th April 2003

1. Following comments made by various junior members of staff, I would like to emphasize that the memo of 1st April regarding use of "peel and seal" envelopes was not an April Fool's Day joke. Perpetration of such jokes is not amusing to the victim and severely forbidden under council rules.

2. We have noted that the preferred nomenclature for staff is "lick and stick" rather than the more formal term used in the previous memo. The more modern term will thus be used in any further correspondence.

3. Note that anyone continuing to use "lick and stick" style envelopes will be disobeying council orders and will be subject to disciplinary procedure.

4. Further attached is printout C01_2003001_ALL_DEPARTMENTS_ 0000000002, a transcript of the information held within this communication for reference should any dispute arise. If you feel that the transcript does not truly reflect this communication you must query the matter with the Council Monitoring Department.

5. If you have any queries regarding this matter you must quote the reference above when contacting us.

E M Frost

Senior Administrator

To: The Senior Administrator
Malbury Centre Health Clinic
43 Green Lanes
Malbury WS2 HH5
7th April 2003

Dear Senior Administrator Valerie Grateley

Thank you for your letter of 04/04/2003.

There seems to be a little confusion over my last letter regarding the two codes created vis-à-vis my original query regarding Glazing Maintenance Project, Reference KL/000001/AE/9/4.3.

When I wrote "the latter one needs to be cancelled" I did not realise that this would be translated as "cancel both applications".

I apologise for any confusion which may inadvertently and fully understandably have been caused by my use of the word "one" which obviously is clearly open to misinterpretation and could be read as "two or more or any number up to and possibly including whatever you first thought of".

In order to eliminate all possible confusion, could you re-open the application under the code ALLBRIGHTJIM2003_0000000001? No other, just that one.

Incidentally, could you please send me a Claim For Expenses Form form?

Yours Faithfully

Jim Allbright

J Allbright
32 Pinetree Road
Malbury WS9 JG8

To: The Administrator
Malbury Centre Health Clinic
43 Green Lanes
Malbury WS2 HH5

7th April 2003

Dear Sandi pp The Administrator

Enclosed please find completed Claim For Expenses Form in the standard sealed envelope. I've decided to charge this one to "Administration Administration". At first I thought that was a typo, but it looks like they do have a category for administering administration. And why not?

This week it's a Chinese takeaway menu for your records. I can recommend the Spring Rolls, but watch out for anything with pork in it.

Could you please send me another Claim For Expenses Form form?

Yours Faithfully

Jim Allbright

J Allbright
32 Pinetree Road
Malbury WS9 JG8

P.S.

Hi Sandi

Funny, that, about your ex-fiancé. When I was still a copper, a mate and I went around to arrest someone like that. Silly bugger tried to leg it and fell down some stairs, broke his leg. The first thing he does is claim that we pushed him, trying to get out of the trial or something, god knows. Didn't do him any good - the jury found him guilty and he got five years. That was the going rate at the time.

Didn't do me any good either. There was an official investigation and the psychiatrist decided that I was suffering from post stress traumatic disorder because I'd had a beer bottle shoved in my face a few weeks before. The bosses were going through one of their paranoia cycles, almost telling us not to nick anyone just in case they sued us for being unpleasant. So the trick cyclist's theory was very handy - they didn't have to decide whether I had pushed the little scroat, just advise that I took retirement on health grounds. It wasn't a suggestion, either. Retirement? As if I was even close to retirement age! I reckon I must be the youngest retired person ever.

Still the pension's pretty good. The window-cleaning job brings in quite a bit as well. You'd be surprised how much you can charge. And it's nice relaxing work in the open, and people don't attack you with beer bottles. And you don't have psychiatrists asking you strange questions about your childhood and your mother.

Jim

P.P.S.

(Or have I missed one?) Sounds like your Graham is the only one who has a clue. I'd tell him not to let them wind him up though, that just means they've won. He has to learn to use the system.

Know what they've done this time? Some idiot called Valerie something or other thought that my application hadn't been dealt with, so she creates a

52

new account, or whatever you call these things, on the system. So I write to her explaining that everything was fine, can she cancel the second account. The first account is called ALLBRIGHTJIM 2003_ 00 00000001, the second is ALLBRIGHTJAMES 2003_0000000001. Only she's only gone and cancelled both now.

I've written to her asking her to re-open the ALLBRIGHT JIM2003_ 0000000001 one. I'm not going to hold my breath, she'll probably end up re-opening the wrong one.

P.P.P.S.

Okay, I'll admit it. What I know about star signs you could write on the back of a postage stamp and still have space for the national anthem. All I know is that I'm definitely one of the good guys.

Definitely.

Malbury Council Accounts Department

Malbury Council Centre, Park Road, Malbury, WS8 HT9

To: J Allbright

32 Pinetree Road

Malbury WS9 JG8

Reference Code : ALLBRIGHTJIM2003_0000000001

7th April 2003

1. Notification of payment

Details : Refund of Fixed Penalty Fine payment due to closure of account, breakdown attached

2. Payee : Jim Allbright

3. Account details : As specified in breakdown

4. Date of payment : 04/04/2003

5. Amount : £213.46 (Twenty Pounds and thirteen pence)

6. Accruals : £5 (Five Pounds) per calendar month of non-payment

7. Accrual Basis : Monthly interest

8. Method of Payment : Electronic Transfer

9. Contest : If you wish to contest this payment you must contact Malbury Services Auditing Department. This Department is unable to enter into any correspondence with you over this matter.

10. Declaration : This payment has been automatically generated by our computer services. The amounts may not be muddified.

Malbury Council Accounts Department

To Anonymous

Malbury Council Fines Services

Malbury Council Centre , Park Road , Malbury WS8 HT9

9th April 2003

Dear Anonymous Fine Repayment Person

Yes, I know you said in your letter that I shouldn't contact you, but I would like to point out to you that you have still not given me the address of your Auditing Department, so I'm afraid you'll have to do.

Thank you very, very much for refunding the amount of the fine, it's extremely kind, nay, generous, of you to be so prompt, especially as I did not pay the fine in the first place. In fact, I'll let you into a secret, I never had any intention of ever paying it. Yes, I know it's naughty of me, but I guess I'm just that sort of person.

Technically speaking therefore the money does not belong to me. However, since you have failed to send me a Claim For Expenses Form form, I have not been able to invoice the council for work involved in dealing with the original paperwork, so I will be claiming the amount you have sent as part-payment for that work.

Anytime you wish to refund money I haven't paid for fines issued for something I didn't do, feel free to refund as much as you want. Refund away!

Incidentally, could you please send me a Claim For Expenses Form form?

Yours Faithfully

Jim Allbright

J Allbright

32 Pinetree Road

Malbury WS9 JG8

P.S. Are you in fact an alien from another planet?

I can't wait to see what incomprehensible thing you are going to do next.

Oh, whoops, I should have put that PS on a separate page. Too late now. My bad, as I believe the youngsters say these days.

Malbury Council Senior Management

Internal E-Mail

From : P V Hamilton,

To : J C Thornton

Sent : 11:32 9th April 2003

Jane

Had an ear-wigging from that poxy idiot from the Malbury Residents' Association about the state of the window at the clinic in Green Lanes. Apparently it needs cleaning. Can you get someone to get it sorted? Probably some sloppy organisation on the part of one of the clerks. Or maybe the window cleaner's just a lazy sod.

Thanks
Pete
Senior Manger

To: J Allbright

32 Pinetree Road

Malbury WS9 JG8

Reference Code : ALLBRIGHTJIM2003_0000000001

Project Code : KL/000001/AE/9/4.3.

9th April 2003

1. It has come to my attention as project manager of the above project that you have closed your application account tender for the contract for the project. Our records do not show the reason for this. Enclosed find form ACC20030409_3.5, Account Cancellation Reason. I have also enclosed pre-addressed and stamped envelope L465H23 to be used when returning the form. Note that the size of the envelope is a temporary measure.

2. Further enclosed is printout R22_20030303_ ALLBRIGHTJIM2003_0-000000004, a transcript of the information held within this communication for reference should any dispute arise. If you feel that the transcript does not truly reflect this communication you must query the matter with the Council Monitoring Department.

3. If you have any queries regarding this matter you must quote the reference above when contacting us.

J C Thornton

J C Thornton

Project Manager

P.S.

Dear Jim (if I may be allowed to be so informal)

I am sure I am not breaching commercial confidence by saying that your application was definitely one of the better ones we have received. Malbury Council Project Services are aware of the dangers of false economy and of paying too low a rate for substandard work. The project in question is being re-evaluated in order to bring the remuneration component in line with the professional standards we require for a project of this visibility. I am sure I can tell you without breaking confidentiality rules that an application from yourself would be looked upon favourably.

Regards

Jane (Thornton)

Malbury Council Project Services

Malbury Council Centre, Park Road, Malbury, WS8 HT9

To: J Allbright

32 Pinetree Road

Malbury WS9 JG8

Reference Code : ALLBRIGHTJAMES2003_0000000001

Project Code : KL/000001/AE/9/4.3.

9th April 2003

1. It has come to my attention as project manager of the above project that you have closed your application account tendering for the contract for the project. Our records do not show the reason for this. Enclosed please find form ACC20030409_3.5, Account Cancellation Reason. I have also enclosed pre-addressed and stamped envelope L465H23 to be used when returning the form. Please note that the size of the envelope is a temporary measure.

2. Further enclosed is printout R22_20030303_ ALLBRIGHTJAMES2003_- 0000000001, a transcript of the information held within this communication for reference should any dispute arise. If you feel that the transcript does not truly reflect this communication you must query the matter with the Council Monitoring Department.

3. If you have any queries regarding this matter you must quote the reference above when contacting us.

J C Thornton

J C Thornton

Project Manager

P.S.

Dear James (if I may be allowed to be so informal)

I am sure I am not breaching commercial confidence by saying that your application was definitely one of the better ones we have received. Malbury Council Project Services are aware of the dangers of false economy and of paying too low a rate for substandard work. The project in question is being re-evaluated in order to bring the remuneration component in line with the professional standards we require for a project of this visibility. I am sure I can tell you without breaking confidentiality rules that an application from yourself would be looked upon favourably.

Regards

Jane (Thornton)

Malbury Council Project Services

Internal Memo

To All Departments

9th April 2003

1. As you all know the new computer system installed a few months ago was designed to increase efficiency and reduce costs. To a large extent our hard work in this complex area has been extremely successful, and I would like to say a vote of thanks to all involved who put so much work and positive effort into the project despite the tough deadlines and extreme complexity of the project.

2. However one area stands out as being a problem, and that is the amount of paper we find ourselves purchasing. Our original calculations proved that we would save at least twenty per cent (20%) of paper consumption. These figures are still valid, and we have been conducting investigations as to the reason for the high consumption.

3. After exhaustive analysis we have come to the unfortunate conclusion that, while the majority of employees are loyally doing their best to conserve resources, a small minority are utilising Council resources for their own private use. I must remind you that this is against Council Rules and is a sackable offence.

4. It has been decided therefore that all paper requirements must be submitted through this department until further notice. A form is attached for this purpose. Please note that amounts requested must be submitted as the number of pages required. Paper will no longer be issued in packs. You must ensure that all requests are received by this department at least a week before the required date.

5. Further attached is printout P01_2003001_ALL_DEPARTMENTS_ 0000001742, a transcript of the information held within this communication for reference should any dispute arise. If you feel that the transcript does not truly reflect this communication you must query the matter with the Council Monitoring Department.

6. If you have any queries regarding this matter you must quote the reference above when contacting us.

J C Thornton

Project Manager

Malbury Centre Health Clinic

43 Green Lanes, Malbury, WS2 HH5

To:J Allbright

32 Pinetree Road

Malbury WS9 JG8

Reference Code : ALLBRIGHTJIM2003_0000000001

10th April 2003

1. Thank you for your letter concerning Glazing Maintenance Project, Reference KL/000001/AE/9/4.3.

2. I have passed your comments on to our Auditing Department as required by Council rules. In order to comply with the Data Protection Act and European Union laws your name was not included in the communication, only the reference code.

3. As per your request I enclose Form ACC985, Claim For Expenses. You must return the form in the pre-paid envelope.

4. Further enclosed is printout R76_20030303_ ALLBRIGHTJIM2003_0-000000008, a transcript of the information held within this communication for reference should any dispute arise. If you feel that the transcript does not truly reflect this communication you must query the matter with the Council Monitoring Department.

5. If you have any queries regarding this matter you must quote the reference above when contacting us.

S Goodwin

pp The Administrator

P.S.

Dear Jim

Sorry about this page and the awful handwriting, but I had to tear something from an old exercise book. They've decided we have to sign for every single sheet of paper we use now. Can you imagine?

Funny that, the bloke I was going to marry - can't even think of him as my fiancé, these days - he was thrown down some stairs by a couple of coppers. Just a pity they didn't do a proper job of it. The bloke you nicked wasn't called Wayne Hammond was he?

Hope your face wasn't too hurt - what is it about blokes that they want to pick a fight when they've had a few? And they always seem to think a bottle is a good weapon. Graham does je-jootsi, or some martial arts thing. He reckons a weapon is usually more dangerous to the person holding it. He's been in a funny mood recently. We went out for drinks the other evening after work, we were talking about something or other - this war, it was, and how some people seem so anti it and others think it's such a good thing. He said something like "people only read what they want to see, not what's actually been said", and then he had a fit of the giggles. He can be strange.

He told me something which explained something I thought was odd : before they introduced this new system Dr Singh used to see loads of patients, sometimes thirty or forty a day, only now that the appointments are scheduled centrally for all practices he only sees about four in the whole day. I thought it was because the system was working so well - that's what they told us, anyway. Turns out that the system rejects most of them, or schedules them for next year, or last year, or even for Dr Howard's practice, and that closed down six months ago. Some patients still turn up without an appointment, so they've employed two security guards - if you don't have an appointment, or a security pass, you don't get in. How madder can they get? Two burly blokes threatening sick old people with being arrested if they don't go away? Dr Singh is thinking about moving his desk outside, but that would probably only get him into trouble - you can hardly ask someone to strip in the middle of the street, can you? (When I pointed that out to him he got a funny look in his eyes and said, 'Yes, why not? We will make a revolution!')

Sandi

xxx

P.P.S.

The idiot called Valerie who closed your accounts down also works here, in the afternoons, she's at head office mornings - we've got five staff and one doctor; two receptionists, a cleaner, me and Valerie (who calls herself a project manager, her title is Senior Administrator, no-one knows what she's supposed to be) - that's not counting the security guards. Valerie is a right cow, by the way, thinks she's a right little miss muck; if you criticise any of the daft ideas they have at the council offices she only spends half an hour lecturing you about how they know best and we must do as they say, be positive, blah-blah-bloody-throw-up-blah. She actually thinks this idea of signing a piece of paper to get another piece of paper will save costs! Would you believe she actually insists on checking that I've only used the number of sheets of paper I've asked for?

P.P.P.S.

So are you going out with anyone yet? Anyone special turned up in your life, as they say? I'm glad I got rid of Rory, but sometimes it feels a bit lonely. Though Helen is great fun of course.

What sort of car do you drive?

To: The Project Manager
Malbury Council Project Services
Malbury Council Centre
Park Road
Malbury WS8 HT9

11th April 2003

Dear Project Manager J C Thornton

Many thanks for your letters of 09/04/2003. As I have informed your Senior Administrator Valerie Grateley, there were two accounts opened for my application, ALLBRIGHTJIM2003_0000000001 and ALLBRIGHTJAMES2003_0000000001.

The latter I believe to be a mistake due to overzealous oversight.

If we could have the second one closed, and the first reopened, all should be well.

Thank you for being so positive about my application. I do try to be professional about these matters, and I had been a little concerned about the low priority such an important project had been given as far as financial investment is concerned.

May I also say that your printouts have that same indefinable air, a kind of quality, almost sensuous in the order and firmness.

Incidentally, could you please send me a Claim For Expenses Form form?

Yours Faithfully

Jim Allbright

J Allbright
32 Pinetree Road
Malbury WS9 JG8

Malbury Council Project Services

Malbury Council Centre, Park Road, Malbury, WS8 HT9

To: J Allbright

32 Pinetree Road

Malbury WS9 JG8

Reference Code : ALLBRIGHTJAMES2003_0000000001

Project Code : KL/000001/AE/9/4.3.

14th April 2003

1. Thank you for your letter concerning Glazing Maintenance Project, Reference KL/000001/AE/9/4.3.

2. I am glad to note that the slight misunderstanding was caused due to enthusiastic work by our Senior Administrator V Grateley rather than sloppiness which unfortunately still can be seen in some of the junior staff, a situation we are continually striving to address.

3. I have instructed the relevant personnel to reactivate your account.

4. I enclose as per your request a Claim For Expenses Form form. Note that the size of the envelope is a temporary measure.

5. I have passed your comments on to our Auditing Department as required by Council rules. In order to comply with the Data Protection Act and European Union laws your name was not included in the communication, only the reference code.

6. Further enclosed is printout R22_20030303_ALL BRIGHTJAMES2003_- 0000000002, a transcript of the information held within this communication for reference should any dispute arise. If you feel that the transcript does not truly reflect this or wonder why her husband tells her he's working late when he's getting pissed in the Rat and Carrot because he can't stand her you must query the matter with the Council Monitoring Department or possibly her old man because he has better jokes though this project is the biggest joke I've ever seen.

If you have any queries regarding this matter you must quote the reference above when contacting us.

J C Thornton

J C Thornton

Project Manager

P.S.

Dear James (I hope you don't mind my being informal in this private addendum)

Thank you very much for your professional evaluation of my handling of this project. I find it regrettable that so few seem to understand the level of quality required for such projects. When we have all council employees paying the same attention to detail for every project, as we have for this one, I believe we will have achieved the level of efficiency commensurate with large organisations in the public sector which share our budgetary levels, but, sadly, surpass us in levels of efficiency.

It is good to know that there are others who share our aim of "lean and clean" as I like to term it.

Regards

Jane

Malbury Centre Health Clinic

43 Green Lanes, Malbury, WS2 HH5

To: J Allbright
32 Pinetree Road
Malbury WS9 JG8
Reference Code : ALLBRIGHTJIM2003_0000000002

15th April 2003

1. Thank you for your letter concerning Glazing Maintenance Project, Reference KL/000001/AE/9/4.3. We have opened a new account for you as requested.

2. I have enclosed the forms required for tender. Note that, in accordance of Council implementation of the Data Protection Act, we are not permitted to see some of the forms, and these must be sealed in the envelopes provided before being returned. They will be forwarded to the relevant auditing departments.

3. The data requested is essential for the monitoring of contracts issued by Malbury Council in order to ensure that they comply with the Equal Opportunity and other Acts of Parliament.

4. Enclosed find :

Form RI654/A/V/4.5.2C : Personal Details. To be sealed in envelope marked L421H70

Form PFG-143-RN2#1A : Cultural Background. To be sealed in envelope marked L421H71

Form X10000.A : Sexual and Religious Details. To be sealed in envelope marked L421H72

Form N98 : Other Details. To be sealed in envelope marked K56H1

Form YJ76E : Details of tender - this does not need to be enclosed in a sealed envelope.

5. You must return the completed forms in their sealed envelopes inside the pre-paid envelope enclosed, along with form YJ76E.

6. Do not include any personal details other than in the relevant sealed envelope.

7. Further enclosed is printout R76_20030303_ALLBRIGHTJIM2003_2 _0000000001, a transcript of the information held within this communication for reference should any dispute arise. If you feel that the transcript does not truly reflect this communication you must query the matter with the Council Monitoring Department.

8. Note that all correspondence must be addressed to 'The Administrator'. Council policy does not permit the use of titles such as Sir or Madam, in order to avoid potential gender bias.

9. If you have any queries regarding this matter you must quote the reference above when contacting us.

S Goodwin

pp The Administrator

P.S.

Dear Jim

Sorry about all the forms and stuff again. The system
won't allow us just to reopen an old account. We've got to
start everything from scratch, security, they tell us.
Load of wotsits if you ask me.

Sometimes you just feel like giving up.

Sandi

Malbury Centre Health Clinic Senior Administrators' Department

43 Green Lanes, Malbury, WS2 HH5

To: J Allbright

32 Pinetree Road

Malbury WS9 JG8

Reference Code : ALLBRIGHTJAMES2003_0000000002

15th April 2003

1. Thank you for your letter concerning Glazing Maintenance Project, Reference KL/000001/AE/9/4.3. We have opened a new account for you as requested. For security reasons, and to enhance the overall service we supply and simplify the tendering process your old account cannot be reopened.

2. We are required to implement council policy of avoiding misuse of potentially derogatory use of language. A committee directive has been issued banning the use of the phrase "window cleaning" as possibly offensive. The facilities required of the project are those of maintaining a hygienic and clear state of the street facing glass frontage of Malbury Centre Health Clinic, measuring approximately 5 metres by two, including the door. The full description of the project requirements are enclosed.

3. I have enclosed the forms required for tender. Please note that, in accordance of Council implementation of the Data Protection Act, we are not permitted to see some of the forms, and these must be sealed in the envelopes provided before being returned. They will be forwarded to the relevant auditing departments.

4. The data requested is essential for the monitoring of contracts issued by Malbury Council in order to ensure that they comply with the Equal Opportunity and other Acts of Parliament.

5. Enclosed find :

Form RI654/A/V/4.5.2C : Personal Details. To be sealed in envelope marked L421H70

Form PFG-143-RN2#1A : Cultural Background. To be sealed in envelope marked L421H71

Form X10000.A : Sexual and Religious Details. To be sealed in envelope marked L421H72

Form N98 : Other Details. To be sealed in envelope marked K56H1

Form YJ76E : Details of tender - this does not need to be enclosed in a sealed envelope.

6. You must return the completed forms in their sealed envelopes inside the pre-paid envelope enclosed, along with form YJ76E.

7. Do not include any personal details other than in the relevant sealed envelope.

8. Further enclosed is printout R76_20030303_ ALLBRIGHT JAMES2003_- 2_0000000001, a transcript of the information held within this communication for reference should any dispute arise. If you feel that the transcript does not truly reflect this communication you must query the matter with the Council Monitoring Department. Or alternatively you might like to piss into the wind as it will do you as much good.

9. Note that all correspondence must be addressed to 'The Administrator'. Council policy does not permit the use of titles such as Sir or Madam, in order to avoid potential gender bias. Please do not use phrases such as prize tit, it only upsets people.

10. If you have any queries regarding this matter you must quote the reference above when contacting us.

V Grateley

V Grateley

Senior Administrator

P.S.

Dear James (if I may call you that)

I can confidently say that your tender has a strong chance of succeeding. There is only one other tender, and that is being handled by a junior grade who unfortunately shows no inclination to achieve the high standards we are all aiming for.

Yours Sincerely

Valerie Grateley

P.P.S.

Like the paper? We're all doing our best to conserve resources, so I thought I'd use up some old stock of lavender blue which was bought ages ago, and no-one ever uses any more.

To: The Administrator

Malbury Centre Health Clinic

43 Green Lanes

Malbury WS2 HH5

20th April 2003

Dear Sandi pp The Administrator

Enclosed please find completed Claim For Expenses Form in the standard sealed envelope, plus all the other fascinating forms. I know it's not really up to me to comment, but don't you think those large envelopes are a bit of a waste of money?

Could you please send me another Claim For Expenses Form form?

Yours Faithfully

Jim Allbright

J Allbright

32 Pinetree Road

Malbury WS9 JG8

P.S.

Dear Sandi

When I got all those forms again I couldn't believe my eyes. Then I just fell about laughing. Well, you have to, don't you? I took them down the pub yesterday lunch time, and a group of us had a great time filling them in. I can't repeat their suggestions for such questions as "Gender bias", and it was only through strong discipline that I managed to avoid answering "Planet Zog" as "Ethnic Origin", mainly because I reckon that the people who dreamed up this stuff just for a window cleaning job must be from Planet Zog. They might think I was one of their relatives and ask if I knew when the next flying saucer was due.

Main reason I went down the pub, apart from needing a drink to do the forms, was the weather - bloody ridiculous. Good Friday was lovely, a real scorcher. Saturday it was like winter all over again. Some places even had snow, they say.

Jim

P.P.S.

Are you seriously saying that you have to sign a piece of paper for every piece of paper you use? Maybe I have a simple view of things, but doesn't that automatically double the amount?

P.P.P.S.

Yes, that was his name now you mention it, Wayne Hammond. Also known as Wayne David, David Waine, Waine Roberts, Robert Wayne - you get the drift. Charming bugger, I'll give him that, but robbing from naive old people is unforgivable in my book. Pity the stairs weren't higher. And steeper. With a brick wall at the end. We could have bounced him off it a few times.

I was hardly scratched by that bottle, bloke was too pissed to try anything serious. Your Graham's right as far as that goes - the bloke who had a go at me almost fell over onto his own bottle. If my mate hadn't caught him he could have had some nasty injuries. Maybe they should bring back National Service - let the young thugs have their fights in some other country.

I wouldn't worry about Graham having fits of the giggles - these computer geeks seem to live in their heads, can't see it does any good, they need to get out more, but at least they don't go around attacking defenceless old people. Then again, those ones who create these viruses, I reckon they need a good hiding.

What you said about Dr Singh only getting a few patients a day - that was interesting. Seems to me these days all the politicians are interested in is in fiddling the figures. They don't mind if people are dying on the streets - not in their streets, mind - so long as the figures show that everything is tickety-boo. Strange world we live in where people can point at a number and believe in it while you can see with your own eyes that it's wrong. What was that quote about statistics being lies?

Your Valerie The Moo has done it again - re-opened the ALLBRIGHTJAMES account, or to be more accurate, created a new one, which means all the same forms. I've just copied the responses from one lot to the other.

Let me get this straight : are you saying that you have one doctor and five support staff in the Clinic?

I'm still not going out with anyone at the moment - got a bit used to living on my own, really, I can go to the pub if I feel like it, have meals if and when I feel like it, that sort of stuff. As for my car, it's a rather beaten up van, the one I use for the job. Might not look like much, but all the important things - engine, brakes, tyres, lights - are in excellent nick. I'm quite fond of the old girl, really. She's reliable, dependable, and doesn't complain if I stay out late. What more can a bloke ask for?

To: The Senior Administrator
Malbury Centre Health Clinic
43 Green Lanes
Malbury WS2 HH5

20th April 2003

Dear Senior Administrator Valerie Grateley

Thank you for your letter of 05/04/2003.

I have completed the forms and sealed them in their relevant envelopes, enclosed with this one.

I know it's not really my business, but I see you have sent the old envelopes, the ones you have to lick before sealing. I was under the impression that these had been replaced by larger ones which didn't need the licking bit.

Thank you also for your kind words regarding the likely success of my tender. I must also add that the lavender blue paper is very impressive, it has a certain quality of control without surrendering what could be termed an essential femininity. And it is good to know that you are utilising old stocks of paper to avoid waste.

Could you please send me another Claim For Expenses Form form?

Yours Faithfully

James Allbright

J Allbright
32 Pinetree Road
Malbury WS9 JG8

Malbury Centre Health Clinic

43 Green Lanes, Malbury, WS2 HH5

To: J Allbright

32 Pinetree Road

Malbury WS9 JG8

Reference Code : ALLBRIGHTJIM2003_0000000002

24th April 2003

1. Thank you for your letter concerning Glazing Maintenance Project, Reference KL/000001/AE/9/4.3.

2. New council rules require all staff and contractors to Malbury Council to undergo a medical examination prior to any contractual or employment agreement(s). An appointment has been automatically generated for you to see Dr J Singh at Malbury Centre Health Clinic on

3. 05/05/2003.

4. Exact details are attached.

5. If you cannot attend the scheduled appointment please contact Malbury Council Project Services in writing before

6. 01/05/2003.

7. You must not contact the Clinic directly, as appointment scheduling is carried out centrally for all clinics.

8. I have passed your comments on to our Auditing Department as required by Council rules. In order to comply with the Data Protection Act and European Union laws your name was not included in the communication, only the reference code.

9. As per your request I enclose Form ACC985, Claim For Expenses. You must return the form in the pre-paid envelope.

10. Further enclosed is printout R76_20030303_ALLBRIGHT JIM2003_2_0000000002, a transcript of the information held within this communication for reference should any dispute arise. If you feel that the transcript does not truly reflect this communication you must query the matter with the Council Monitoring Department.

11. If you have any queries regarding this matter you must quote the reference above when contacting us.

S Goodwin

pp The Administrator

P.S. Dear Jim

Know what you mean about the forms. Apparently this new system is designed to analyse all the different figures so they can tell how many different ethnic groups, as they call them, lesbians, gays, over-fifties, under-twenties, you name it, have been employed on council contracts. They have to meet some quota which reflects the national average (that's a quote by the way). As far as I can see the national averages don't even agree, and anyway, it doesn't make sense to use the national average, there are loads fewer, Jamaicans, say, here than there are in London or anywhere else. I mean, what if there was only one lesbian Jamaican in the area and the statistimitics said they had to employ five? Poor woman would have to do overtime.

You're right about the weather last weekend. Easter weekend, I took Helen to Margate as a treat, had to save up for ages for the train fare, trains were crowded, late, dirty, weather was perishing, Helen was unhappy. She isn't old enough to understand why it isn't sunny every day, poor little thing. Still, I managed to cheer her up a little. We walked on the pavement next to the beach, skipping and dancing, singing a silly little song we made up ourselves. Had an ice-cream, she likes those. So do I, come to it.

Yes, one form for each individual little piece of paper. Might seem obvious to you, me and anyone with half a brain cell, but I reckon this lot lost the plot somewhere. They go on these funny courses, juggling balls, play-acting, 'bonding', then come back thinking that they know everything and everyone else knows nothing. And those courses are expensive!

So you mean you're carrying on with both applications? That should be fun. Maybe you should send letters from the JIM account saying that the JAMES one is dodgy or something, and vice versa. That'd confuse them no end. Especially seeing as you're the only person who has applied. Well, when I say you're the only one, we had some enquiries from people who thought it was a job installing windows, and one who thought it was a nursing job!

Yes, one doctor, five support staff, no nurses, plus two security guards. If it wasn't for the moo we could get all our work done in an hour, close the clinic and go home, instead we spend most of our time with these bloody forms!

I think you should find yourself a girlfriend. Every man needs a woman, just like every woman really needs a man. Though knowing my luck with blokes, I wonder if I'll ever find Mr Right. Even Mr Close-To-Right-With-Only-A-Few-Irritating-Habits would do me. Most blokes run a mile when they hear you've got a kid.

Sandi xxx

P.P.S. Did you see I got the computer to make your appointment in the right year? It wasn't easy, you know. And I know you don't really need a medical, but it's a new rule they've dreamed up. And it means we'll get to meet at last. Can't wait!

Malbury Centre Health Clinic Senior Administrators' Department

43 Green Lanes, Malbury, WS2 HH5

To:J Allbright
32 Pinetree Road
Malbury WS9 JG8
Reference Code : ALLBRIGHTJAMES2003_0000000002

24th April 2003

To : J Allbright

1. Thank you for your letter concerning Glazing Maintenance Project, Reference KL/000001/AE/9/4.3.

2. I must apologise for the old-style "lick-and-stick" envelopes which were sent out due to an error by a junior clerk. I have arranged for the envelopes and their contents to be destroyed by our trained operatives of the Malbury Disposals Department.

3. Because the forms have had to be destroyed I am including a new set, with the approved-style "peel-and-seal" envelopes.

4. Due to the dangers of the old-style envelopes it is the responsibility of Malbury Council to ensure that you have not suffered any physical or mental harm from the use thereof. I have thus arranged an appointment for you to see Dr J Singh at Malbury Centre Health Clinic on

5. 05/05/2003.

6. Exact details are attached.

7. If you cannot attend the scheduled appointment you must contact Malbury Council Project Services in writing before

8. 01/05/2003.

9. You must not contact the Clinic directly, as appointment scheduling is carried out centrally for all clinics.

10. I have enclosed the forms required for tender. Note that, in accordance of Council implementation of the Data Protection Act, we are not permitted to see some of the forms, and these must be sealed in the envelopes provided before being returned. They will be forwarded to the relevant auditing departments.

82

11. The data requested is essential for the monitoring of contracts issued by Malbury Council in order to ensure that they comply with the Equal Opportunity and other Acts of Parliament.

12. Enclosed find :

Form RI654/A/V/4.5.2C : Personal Details. To be sealed in envelope marked L421H70

Form PFG-143-RN2#1A : Cultural Background. To be sealed in envelope marked L421H71

Form X10000.A : Sexual and Religious Details. To be sealed in envelope marked L421H72

Form N98 : Other Details. To be sealed in envelope marked K56H1

Form YJ76E : Details of tender - this does not need to be enclosed in a sealed envelope.

13. You must return the completed forms in their sealed envelopes inside the pre-paid envelope enclosed, along with form YJ76E.

14 You must not include any personal details other than in the relevant sealed envelope.

15. Further enclosed is printout R76_20030303_ ALLBRIGHTJAMES2003_- 2_0000000002, a transcript of the information held within this communication for reference should any dispute arise. If you feel that the transcript does not truly reflect this communication you must query the matter with the Council Refuse Department.

16. Note that all correspondence must be addressed to 'The Administrator'. Council policy does not permit the use of titles such as Bum or Turnip face, in order to avoid potential gender bias.

17. If you have any queries regarding this matter you must quote your shoe size when contacting us.

V Grateley

V Grateley

Senior Administrator

WS2 HH5

P.S.

Dear James

Thank you for your kind words regarding my handling of this project. Something I should have mentioned previously : please do not reply to anything I say in these personal addenda in your main letter. Everything in the main part of the letter is input into our computer system, and if there was any record of my discussing the tender with you certain people might read more into that than the innocent social exchange it is. Unfortunately there are many people in the world today who are willing to mis-read things, or even read something that isn't there.

I do like the lavender blue paper. I agree entirely about the feminine aspect, something which appears sadly to have disappeared from modern life. I don't want to give you the idea that I'm some complaining old grandmother, far from it, I haven't even reached thirty yet, but I am sure the world would be a better place if women maintained their femininity rather than trying to be "one of the lads", drinking all night, swearing, and all the rest of the terrible habits you can't fail to notice these days. You only have to look at the number of single mothers living on benefits to see how low things have gone. Seeing some of them, you can understand why their partners left them. It is such a sad reflection on those of us who have proved that women can work and succeed in modern life just as well as men.

I see you have your own company. I have always admired independent people. I'm thinking of starting my own consultancy one day - if you have any tips on that I'd be most grateful.

I think I shall make this lavender paper my company's official colour. There's boxes of it here waiting to be used, it would only go to waste otherwise. What do you think?

Yours Sincerely

Valerie Grateley

To: The Administrator
Malbury Centre Health Clinic
43 Green Lanes
Malbury WS2 HH5

27th April 2003

Dear Sandi pp The Administrator

Thank you for arranging the medical appointment. I presume that financial outlay in terms of petrol and time can be charged via the standard Claim For Expenses Form form?

Enclosed please find the usual completed Claim For Expenses Form form in the standard sealed envelope.

Could you please send me another Claim For Expenses Form form?

Yours Faithfully

Jim Allbright

J Allbright
32 Pinetree Road
Malbury WS9 JG8

P.S.

Dear Sandi

We had the same problem in the force with quotas and gender and race and all the rest. Trouble is they kept blowing hot and cold. One week you weren't allowed to question someone from one of the 'ethnic minorities' (never did understand that phrase) in case he cried "racism", the next we were supposed to go out and nick every single suspect in sight, especially if they were wearing jackets with hoods or sounded foreign.

I'm just glad no-one has thought of asking me whether I wash all windows equally. Do I do as many plain windows as frosted? Have I washed the same number of sash windows as double-glazed? The mind boggles.

I think there's a cosmic law about weather in Britain. If you're working, it's glorious. If you're on holiday it's terrible. Though I must admit that the last time I went to Margate, couple of years ago, it was absolutely glorious. Got quite badly sunburnt, strange to tell.

As far as these funny jaunts the managers go on, same thing happened in the force, senior officers going away to the country for team-building exercises, usual half-baked sociological waffle. Fortunately they decided that plods on the street didn't need team-building. We would have gone on strike, I reckon.

I'll bear the idea in mind, your one about slagging off the other account. Maybe I'll send them an anonymous letter saying that this ALLBRIGHTJAMES bloke uses a bucket made by child slave labour in China. Or is China a good country these days? They keep changing their minds.

If there are five staff plus security guards per one doctor I think I know where my council tax is going!

I shall bear in mind your decree about finding a girlfriend. Trouble is, the ones I meet down the pub, they're either married, sleeping around with everybody, or married and sleeping around with everybody. Not that I'm saying that that's wrong, just that that's not the sort of girlfriend I would prefer.

I wouldn't say I like kids, but they seem to like me for some reason. Guess I learnt how to be firm with them when I was a copper. I think they respect that.

I now have two appointments with Dr Singh for the 5th. Let's hope he has a sense of humour. Oh, and since we'll be meeting for the first time, as you say, I promise to wear a clean shirt. Do you think aftershave on blokes is naff?

Jim

P.P.S.

That was a joke, about the shirt, just in case you think I normally don't wear clean shirts. They might not look like much, but they're always clean.

To: The Senior Administrator
Malbury Centre Health Clinic
43 Green Lanes
Malbury WS2 HH5

27th April 2003

Dear Senior Administrator Valerie Grateley

Thank you for your letter of 24/04/2003.

I have completed the forms and sealed them in their relevant envelopes, enclosed with this one.

These "peel and seal" envelopes are quite big aren't they?

Does the council publish their statistics? That could make interesting reading.

Could you please send me another Claim For Expenses Form form?

Yours Faithfully

James Allbright

J Allbright
32 Pinetree Road
Malbury WS9 JG8

P.S.

Dear Valerie

Sorry about putting the PS stuff into the main letter. I wasn't thinking at the time. Stresses of modern life, always hectic, on the go, you know how it is.

I think if you're going to start your own company you need to do some market research first. Identify your target market, establish whether there is sufficient demand, and if not whether you can create demand. It's quite a technical and complex area if you haven't studied it - some people think it's just charlatans making things up, but you normally find they have never tried it before.

You could also start thinking about the sort of people you would employ. If it's going to be a small company, you must be confident that everyone will get on together. Think about identifying the individuals who will comprise your human resource element, and possibly take them to one of these weekend courses for building team spirit, identify the potential weaknesses and so forth - there are a number of excellent courses available. They are well worth the outlay.

In order to defray financial output you might consider negotiating TV and film rights of the weekend with a television company - "fly on the wall" documentaries are very much in demand these days.

Best of luck

James

Malbury Council Project Services

Internal E-Mail

Private And Confidential

From : J C Thornton, Project Manager, Malbury Council Project Services

To : Peter V Hamilton

Sent : 18:47 28th April 2003

Peter

I've been working on the month-end figures for March - working late again! I know, I shouldn't do it, but we have to get the figures out after all!

As you will recall our analysis of expenditure within the IT department proved that we would attain a 25% saving in paper costs by introducing the Paper Monitoring Scheme. The figures I have received from the various sub-departments indicate that spending on paper has actually increased by 105% - obviously someone hasn't done their sums properly. It seems an unending battle against apathy to get junior staff to pay sufficient attention to detail and accuracy - I hesitate to send out yet another memo highlighting the importance of reliable statistics, but I am afraid it might be necessary. Perhaps a few disciplinary judgements might wake them up.

There isn't time to identify the incorrect figures and have the relevant junior do their work properly, so I propose that, for the moment, we use last month's figures, adjusted by our calculated reduction, duly noted as being provisional until we have time to find out where the error has crept in.

As far as sloppy record keeping goes, I think it would be an idea to set up a sub-committee to analyse the current situation, identify weaknesses, areas for re-evaluation, methods of control and processes to implement. I would suggest that you could be chairperson, and we bring on board Ian Smith,

Project Manager of the Keep Malbury Clean Project, and Vickie Trent, Project Manager of the Malbury Hygiene, Arts, Language and Fire Safety Co-ordinating Committee Project. They are both trained and qualified Project Managers, and can bring a great deal of technical expertise and experienced know-how to such a Project.

Best Regards
Jane

Project Manager
Malbury Council Project Services

Malbury Council Accounts Department

Malbury Council Centre, Park Road, Malbury, WS8 HT9

To: J Allbright

32 Pinetree Road

Malbury WS9 JG8

Reference Code : ALLBRIGHTJIM2003_0000000002

1st May 2003

1. Notification of payment: Details : General expenses payment, breakdown attached

2. Payee : Jim Allbright

3. Account details : As specified in breakdown

4. Date of payment : 31/04/2003

5. Amount : £892.25 (Eight hundred and ninety two pounds and twenty fife pence)

6. Accruals : £None (None)

7. Accrual Basis : Monthly interest

8. Method of Payment : Electronic Transfer

9. Contest : If you wish to contest this payment you must contact Malbury Services Auditing Department. This Department is unable to enter into any correspondence with you over this matter.

10. Declaration : This payment has been automatically generated by our computer services. The amounts may not be muddified.

Malbury Council Accounts Department

Malbury Council Accounts Department

Malbury Council Centre, Park Road, Malbury, WS8 HT9

To: J Allbright

32 Pinetree Road, Malbury, WS9 JG8

Reference Code : ALLBRIGHTJAMES2003_0000000002

1st May 2003

1. Notification of payment: Details : General expenses payment, breakdown attached

2. Payee : James Allbright

3. Account details : As specified in breakdown

4. Date of payment : 31/04/2003

5. Amount : £250.23 (Two hundred and fitfy pounds and twenty three pence)

6. Accruals : £None (None)

7. Accrual Basis : Monthly interest

8. Method of Payment : Electronic Transfer

9. Contest : If you wish to contest this payment you must contact Malbury Services Auditing Department. This Department is unable to enter into any correspondence with you over this matter.

10. Declaration : This payment has been automatically generated by our computer services. The amounts may not be muddified.

Malbury Council Accounts Department

Malbury Centre Health Clinic

43 Green Lanes, Malbury, WS2 HH5

To: J Allbright

32 Pinetree Road

Malbury WS9 JG8

Reference Code : ALLBRIGHTJIM2003_0000000002

6th May 2003

1. Thank you for your letter concerning Glazing Maintenance Project, Reference KL/000001/AE/9/4.3.

2. All expenses incurred in attending medical appointments made by the Council can be recovered using Form ACC985, Claim For Expenses.

3. I have passed your comments on to our Auditing Department as required by Council rules. In order to comply with the Data Protection Act and European Union laws your name was not included in the communication, only the reference code.

4. As per your request I enclose Form ACC985, Claim For Expenses. You must return the form in the pre-paid envelope.

5. Further enclosed is printout R76_20030303_ALLBRIGHTJIM2003_2_0000000003, a transcript of the information held within this communication for reference should any dispute arise. If you feel that the transcript does not truly reflect this communication you must query the matter with the Council Monitoring Department.

6. If you have any queries regarding this matter you must quote the reference above when contacting us.

S Goodwin

pp The Administrator

P.S.

Dear Jim

Sorry I missed you yesterday. Helen was ill, quite badly, poor thing. I had to stay at home to look after her. Typical, the one day I was looking forward to going to work! Still, I'm sure you'll get the job so I'm sure we'll meet up eventually. It feels like I already know you so well. Strange, that, isn't it?

DO, DO, send in a nasty letter about the ALLBRIGHTJAMES account. I like a good laugh. You could make him a gangster or something. Maybe tell them he belongs to the National Front, that would get their knickers in a twist. The old Moo is looking after that account. She'd probably have a fit of the heeby-jeebys.

I'm sure there's a woman out there just right for you, probably desperate to meet you. I don't think a pub is the best place to look for her though - single women just don't go to pubs. Not unless they're in a group, anyway, men seem to think they're looking to be picked up for some reason. I've only been to a pub on my own a couple of times, before Helen was born. I just fancied sitting with a quiet pint and a good book and not being disturbed, but it was like I had a sign over me saying "she fancies a shag with some drunken yob". And ugly, too, and most of them old enough to be my dad, if not my granddad.

I hope my dad didn't do that. Are all men like that? I'm sure Graham isn't like that. Though he does seem a bit strange sometimes. I think he's the first man friend I've had that I haven't actually gone out with. You know, what's that word, platonic. We meet up for drinks almost every Friday these days. One of my neighbours looks after Helen for free - she just likes kids, never had any of her own.

It's good to have someone to have a laugh with. We spend most of the time slagging off the idiots at Council centre. He likes classical music, what kind do you like?

Did you want to have kids when you were married? Do you now?

Sandi

xxx

Malbury Centre Health Clinic Senior Administrators' Department

43 Green Lanes, Malbury, WS2 HH5

To: J Allbright
32 Pinetree Road
Malbury WS9 JG8
Reference Code : ALLBRIGHTJAMES2003_0000000002

6th May 2003

1. Thank you for your letter concerning Glazing Maintenance Project, Reference KL/000001/AE/9/4.3.

2. New council rules require all staff and contractors to Malbury Council to undergo a medical examination prior to any contractual or employment agreement(s). An appointment has been automatically generated for you to see Dr J Singh at Malbury Centre Health Clinic on

3. 14/05/2003.

4. Exact details are attached.

5. Further enclosed is printout R76_20030303_ ALLBRIGHTJAMES2003_- 2_0000000003, a transcript of the information held within this communication for reference should any dispute arise. If you feel that the transcript does not error reflect whoops alert an alien has landed in East Grinstead this communication you must query the matter with the Council Pornographic Collection Department.

6. Note that all correspondence must be addressed to 'The Terminator'. Council policy does not permit the use of titles, in order to avoid potential bender bias.

7. If you have any queries regarding this matter you must quote the book of psalms when contacting us.

V Grateley

V Grateley
Senior Administrator

P.S.

Dear James

You're right about market research. When I did my degree I concentrated on Sociology and Public Relations. It's sad that so many people do not understand the importance of these subjects. They do not seem to be able to grasp that all the really successful companies spend vast amounts on research before deciding on marketing strategies. At least Malbury Council have taken on board a blue-skies approach.

I've also taken on board your points about having the right staff. I've spoken to one of my colleagues, Jane Thornton - you may have received some correspondence from her - and we are pretty confident that we can run a successful consultancy, given our training and experience within project development. We are currently deciding on a name for our company, after which we plan to speak to a headhunting company to ensure we have the best and brightest brains on board. After all, we'll never get to the top if we don't have the best big-hitters with us.

Your suggestion about involving a television company to create a documentary is brilliant. As you point out, it will help defray costs, but even more importantly it will showcase our competency nationwide. I have no doubt that we will be inundated with approaches from top blue-chip companies as soon as the programme premieres.

You are obviously a successful self-made man, and I hesitate to suggest this, but I do believe we could make an extremely successful partnership, yourself, Jane and myself. Please let me know if there's the slightest possibility that you would be prepared to join us as Director of Operations. I will have the post of Director of Projects, Jane will be Director of Marketing and Personnel, so we need an experienced person to run the Operational side of things.

Please let me know what you think.

Yours Sincerely

Valerie

Valerie Grateley

Malbury Council Senior Management

Internal E-Mail

From : P V Hamilton

To : J C Thornton

Sent : 12:45 7th May 2003

Jane

Apologies for not replying sooner about the paper figures, I've been inundated with work recently. This morning I even had to agree to an early round on the golf-course with Sir Henry Walters just to clear some points of policy. Just finished pre-lunch drinks with Councillor Herbert, difficult person to get along with. Now I have to rush off to lunch with Gwendolyn Harris of the Arts Council. It's a hard life, as they say.

The adjustment you made to the monthly figures I leave in your hands as a capable and committed member of staff. I am sure I can rely on you to ensure that we have correct and relevant statistical data as and when we need them.

By all means set up a sub-committee to investigate the problem of junior staff failing to submit correct figures for time-keeping. I will be happy to act as chairman, though with my current hectic schedule it may mean convening for a working breakfast once a week. Albertos Restaurant off Green Street do an excellent breakfast. Process the cost through your expenses as normal.

I'd like to see George Stringham included on the committee. He was complaining only the other day about how difficult it was to find a decent place for breakfast, and he has many good qualities he could bring to bear on any discussion. As my bank manager I know he has that critical approach we so desperately need from the private sector.

Let me know the details when you have the committee structure organised.

By the way, was that you in that rather fetching body-hugging blue dress the other day? Very attractive, I thought.

Peter

Senior Manger

To: The Administrator
Malbury Centre Health Clinic
43 Green Lanes
Malbury WS2 HH5

11th May 2003

Dear Sandi pp The Administrator

Enclosed please find the usual completed Claim For Expenses Form form in the standard sealed envelope

Could you please send me another Claim For Expenses Form form?

Yours Faithfully

Jim Allbright

J Allbright
32 Pinetree Road
Malbury
WS9 JG8

P.S.

Dear Sandi

Sorry to hear about little Helen being sick. Give her a kiss from me. Nothing worse than a poor little unhappy face - especially when its nose is running. Loads of cuddles, that's the best medicine.

Dr Singh and I had a good laugh. I explained about the two appointments and he thought it was hilarious. He said at the start of these new council rules and systems and whatnot he got really stressed. Couldn't do his job properly, hardly saw any patients, that sort of thing. He thought of immigrating to Canada or somewhere, but reckons he's too old, his wife didn't want to, kids have all grown up here, that sort of thing. Eventually he gave up and decided to spend the free time studying for a degree in archaeology. It's been a pet love of his since he was a kid. So we spent an hour discussing archaeology - the medical took about five minutes. Apparently I'm in perfectly good health, good enough to wash windows, anyway. Singh makes archaeology sound fascinating. Maybe I'll take it up as a hobby.

Oh, and I have another appointment with him for Wednesday, which The Moo set up. So I'll see you then.

Getting paid to see a doctor is an interesting way of earning a living. Comes in rather handy at the moment - things are a bit slack these days.

Maybe I will send an anonymous letter to your old cow about that JAMES ALLBRIGHT bloke - should I ask for an expenses form at the same time?

If there is a woman out there just right for me she's keeping herself well hidden. Or maybe you're right about the pub. I shall make an effort to go to an art gallery sometime. I'll be in London next weekend, I'll visit the Tate Modern - I've always wanted to see what the fuss was all about, those cows in formaldehyde and that sort of thing - Modern Art (which, I understand, is different to "modern art", somehow).

It is a pity about single women in pubs. I think you might get away with being on your own in a wine bar, even then I'm not too sure. And I'm sure your dad isn't anything like that. Not all blokes try to pick up anyone in a pub, it's just that you remember the few that do.

I don't mind a bit of classical music now and then. To be honest, I don't listen to music much. Why, I don't know, because when I do remember to put a CD on I enjoy it immensely, whether it's Beethoven or Meat Loaf. Can't say I'm over fond of rap, though, could never get into that sort of stuff. Maybe I've just heard the bad stuff. There was a report in the papers the other day that music companies are complaining that they're getting poor sales results because everyone's nicking the stuff off the internet. Someone else said that their music isn't selling because it's just rubbish - I think that's more likely to be the answer.

Can't say I ever thought about having kids when I was married - the possibility is there in the background, and I suppose you presume you will have kids sometime. Me and the wife - ex-wife - never really talked about it. I don't think she wanted any herself.

Maybe that's why we broke up - not talking to each other. I hear people don't anymore. Sometimes I think I wouldn't mind having someone to come home to. It's great to be able to do what you want when you want, but sometimes you wonder if you aren't missing something.

Jim

The Senior Administrator
Malbury Centre Health Clinic
43 Green Lanes
Malbury WS2 HH5

11th May 2003

Dear Senior Administrator Valerie Grateley

Thank you for your letter of 06/05/2003. Enclosed please find the usual completed Claim For Expenses Form form in the standard sealed envelope

I have made a note in my diary regarding the medical appointment.

Could you please send me another Claim For Expenses Form form?

Yours Faithfully

James Allbright

J Allbright
32 Pinetree Road
Malbury
WS9 JG8

P.S.

Dear Valerie

Thanks for the offer of being Director of Operations in your company-to-be. It's a great honour, but unfortunately I'm already overstretched as it is - you know how it is. Busy all the hours God sends.

When you're deciding on a name for a new company it's important to get it right first time. It has to be simple, memorable and serious, but with a modern touch. You can't allow people to think that you're old-fashioned or out of touch. Something like "The Konzultantz", possibly, which both states what you do and sounds futuristic. When choosing the name for my company "Allbright Cleaners" just stood out.

I presume you've been considering finance. It's best to speak to your financial adviser early on - you're going to have to sell the idea to a bank at some stage. Presentation is everything. Remember, bright colours, the brighter the better. Think pink. Bright pink.

Also worth considering is aiming for an EU grant. There are a number available for research and new companies. I'm sure they'll be fascinated by your plans.

Good luck with the television documentary.

Best of luck

James

P.P.S. How's the bid for the contract doing? Any competition I should be worried about?

Missus V Greatlea Malbury Clinic

Sunday 11 May 2003

Dear Missus Grreatlee

I kno you dont kno me but I want to tell you something about that JAMES ALLBRIGHT. His not a very nice persin. I kno his trying to get a job from you but what you dont kno is his one of those Nazi people, you kno the National Frunt. I wouldnt give him a job if I were you you could end up with egg on your face if the news papers found out.

From a wellwisher

Anonimouse.

P.S. Can I get payed for sending you this infomation?

Malbury Centre Health Clinic Senior Administrators' Department

43 Green Lanes, Malbury, WS2 HH5

To: J Allbright

32 Pinetree Road

Malbury WS9 JG8

Reference Code : ALLBRIGHTJAMES2003_0000000002

15th May 2003

1. Thank you for your letter concerning Glazing Maintenance Project, Reference KL/000001/AE/9/4.3.

2. As per your request I enclose Form ACC985, Claim For Expenses. You must return the form in the pre-paid envelope.

3. Further enclosed is printout R76_20030303_ ALLBRIGHTJAMES2003_- 2_0000000004, a transcript of the local telephone directory for reference should any dispute arise. If you feel that the transcript does not look pretty enough you must query the matter with the Council Calamity Collection Department.

4. Note that all correspondence must be addressed to 'Old Sourpuss'. Council policy does not permit the use of titles such as Mr or Ms, in order to avoid potential glandular bias.

5. If you have any queries regarding this matter you must quote the referee when contacting us.

V Grateley

V Grateley

Senior Administrator

P.S.

Dear James

Yes, I did think there was little chance that you would have the time to join us, but I had to ask. Pity.

Jane and I have been hard at work making policy decisions for our new company. We've agreed that Lavender will be the official colour - pink was definitely an option, but we decided to go for bright lavender instead - it's the sort of thing people will remember. As far as a name goes, I like your suggestion of "The Konzultantz", but Jane thinks it might be too modern. She prefers something like "T&G" for "Thornton and Grateley", but that sounds too much like a trade union to me - after all, it would be absolutely disastrous if people thought we were a trade union of some sort! "G&T" won't do either - could hardly have people thinking we were named after a gin-and-tonic! So if you have any good ideas for a name please let me know.

I've written to the BBC about a documentary - I thought they would have called by now, but I'm told that they have hundreds of letters a week with new programme suggestions, and it takes them a while to get through them all. Patience will have to be a virtue.

Don't worry about the contract. I have heard from one of my own private sources that the other company bidding is run by a member of the British National Party. Malbury Council simply cannot be seen to be endorsing the sort of ideas that they have. Above all we have to be fair and impartial, especially people like myself and Jane, who as unelected officers have an extra duty of care to keep politics out of council contracts.

I've added a note on the system to that file about the person's membership of the BNP. I don't think they will be getting the contract.

Yours Sincerely

Valerie

To: J Allbright

32 Pinetree Road

Malbury WS9 JG8

Reference Code : ALLBRIGHTJIM2003_0000000002

16th May 2003

1. Thank you for your letter concerning Glazing Maintenance Project, Reference KL/000001/AE/9/4.3.

2. As per your request I enclose Form ACC985, Claim For Expenses. You must return the form in the pre-paid envelope.

3. I have passed your comments on to our Auditing Department as required by Council rules. In order to comply with the Data Protection Act and European Union laws your name was not included in the communication, only the reference code.

4. Further enclosed is printout R76_20030303_ALLBRIGHT JIM2003_2_0000000004, a transcript of the information held within this communication for reference should any dispute arise. If you feel that the transcript does not truly reflect this communication you must query the matter with the Council Monitoring Department.

5. If you have any queries regarding this matter you must quote the reference above when contacting us.

S Goodwin

pp The Administrator

P.S. Jim! Jim! Jim!

Damn, damn and damn again! You know what that silly cow The Moo has done this time? Put a note on your file - the JIM one, not the JAMES one - that you're a member of the National Party. Trouble is I can't take it off, something to do with security and access rights. I'll have to ask Graham if he can do something about it, only they say that nobody can change anything on the system apart from the company that made it. I could just kill that bloody cow!

Anyway, what's so bad about the BNP? Everybody makes them out to be Nazis, but I haven't ever seen them walking around wearing swastikas. Never even met one of them to be honest. I reckon it's just the politicians scared of people willing to tell the truth about things.

I missed you on Wednesday as well. Dr Singh told me you'd come for another appointment - he says you must hold a record for someone who isn't ill. I had to go to the local school that Helen's going to be going to soon. She's really looking forward to it. I hope she does well, all I remember about school was trying to get out of it when I was a teenager. We used to go down the shopping centre and stand around waiting for some boys to turn up, or nick makeup and stuff from the shops. Now I wish I'd studied a bit harder, maybe I could have a better job than this one. Still, you never think of that when you're a teenager, do you? Ho, hum.

I used to love buying music before Helen came along - all the latest stuff. Course I wouldn't swap her for the world, but money's tight, so you have to economise - I'd love to have a mobile phone like everyone else, but that would mean not being able to buy things for my little angel. If I was still at school I'd probably shop-lift the stuff again, but I couldn't allow Helen to have a thief as a mother, could I?

My Dad isn't alive any more. Passed away when I was sixteen. I still miss him, he was great fun. And I'm sure he didn't chase after girls in pubs, at least not when he got older. Not that he was that old, of course.

Do you ever see your wife these days? I've read stories where people get divorced and then remarry because they realised they still loved each other. It's only when you have to live with someone you get on each other's nerves, that sort of thing.

Graham's promised to take me out to a real dinner tonight, says I'm suffering from depression and need to get out. Not like a date or anything, he's just the kind that wants to make other people feel better. The neighbour's promised to look after Helen. Haven't been out properly in ages. I'm really looking forward to it. Though Graham can be a bit scary at times. He's incredibly brainy, sometimes I don't know what he's talking about. Then again, I'm not sure he does either.

We must meet up sometime. Soon. I really do want to meet you.

Sandi

xxx

To: The Administrator
Malbury Centre Health Clinic
43 Green Lanes
Malbury WS2 HH5

21st May 2003

Dear Sandi pp The Administrator

Enclosed please find the usual completed Claim For Expenses Form form in the standard sealed envelope.

Could you please send me another Claim For Expenses Form form?

Yours Faithfully

Jim Allbright
J Allbright
32 Pinetree Road
Malbury WS9 JG8

P.S.

Dear Sandi

Well, that'll teach me to do silly things. Even if Graham could remove that note your favourite cow won't forget it. We'll have to see what happens. Maybe I'll sue her for slander or something - libel, I can never remember which is which. I met some of the BNP while I was in the force, not nice people. The ones you see on television wear suits and try to look respectable, but the ones you find in pubs and so on are not the sort of people you want to know.

Sorry to hear about your Dad. Must have been pretty grim, considering how young you were at the time.

As far as Helen goes, that has to be the big question - how do you make teenagers enjoy school? I've often wondered whether teenagers should just be sent away to a camp for a few years - say from thirteen to eighteen. Then they can continue schooling afterwards. From what I remember of schooldays the only reason I wasn't in more trouble is that I managed not to get caught - good training for a policeman. Though I certainly never thought I'd end up joining the force.

Yes, you definitely wouldn't want to get done for shop-lifting. Or anything else for that matter. These days they seem to have lists of anyone and everything - if you go to your local nick to hand in a wallet you've found they probably put you on a list; the "Visited Police Station So Obviously Dodgy" list.

I saw my ex-wife about two years after she'd left me. I'd like to report that she had been dumped by the Turkish carpet seller, but unfortunately she'd dumped him, had found someone else and was very happy. We had a very civilised little chat. Well, we managed not to try to kill each other, anyway.

You have to watch out with these brainy types. I think that sometimes they think too hard and their brain overheats. Tell Graham he needs to take up a hobby.

I did manage to visit the Tate Modern when I was in London. Very strange it was. Some of the exhibits suggest that the artists - if that's what you can call them - had a nasty fixation with, how shall I put this, sexual organs? Some of the other stuff looked more like it was made by piss-artists, probably on drugs as well. Some of it was strangely quite good, if a little weird. And seeing as it was free, I can't really complain. But I didn't meet the woman you keep going on about, and I missed the cow in formaldehyde. Maybe next time.

I am sure we will meet up soon. Maybe we should fix a date rather than missing each other at the clinic every so often. What do you think?

Jim

To: The Senior Administrator

Malbury Centre Health Clinic

43 Green Lanes

Malbury WS2 HH5

21st May 2003

Dear Senior Administrator Valerie Grateley

Thank you for your letter of 06/05/2003. Enclosed please find the usual completed Claim For Expenses Form form in the standard sealed envelope.

Could you please send me another Claim For Expenses Form form?

Yours Faithfully

James Allbright

J Allbright

32 Pinetree Road

Malbury

WS9 JG8

P.S.

Dear Val

You could get in a marketing company to advise you on a company name. It might seem expensive, but it's really an investment. After all, you don't want to find that it means something rude in Japanese when you go multinational. Maybe just one initial - "Q" or something like that. "X" possibly. Get your friends around over a few glasses of wine and have a brain storming session. You'll be surprised at the results. I was wondering whether you only want one colour. Lavender sounds good, but have you considered, say, a mixture of lavender and cream? Bright yellow? You don't want to come across as too single-minded.

Are you sure the other company is run by someone from the BNP? I certainly haven't met anyone like that amongst my numerous contacts. You have to be careful of the Data Protection Act; if he doesn't actually belong to the BNP, and I suspect he doesn't, keeping a note that he does could look nasty in the courts, if you see what I mean.

Good luck

James

Malbury Council Project Services

Internal E-Mail
Private And Confidential
From : J C Thornton
To : Peter V Hamilton

Sent : 08:15 22nd May 2003

Dear Peter

Many thanks for sparing the time to chair the Paper Usage and Record Keeping Evaluation Committee at Albertos yesterday. I never even knew that you could get a vegan egg-and-bacon breakfast. It tasted almost exactly like the way I remember the real thing used to be.

You were definitely right about bringing on board private experience like George Stringham. His analysis of the problem was spot on - the apparent increase in paper usage is due to junior staff including in their reports the paper used for forms requesting paper. Naturally this skews the statistics, as the form paper is not part of our standard usage. I will send out a memo later instructing all staff in the correct counting of paper, i.e. not to include paper used in requesting paper.

And many thanks for referring me to the image consultants HiHo. I've spoken to Vince Spiro and he is confident that they will be able to map out a comprehensive marketing strategy for our new company - or what he calls "the whole package". Their list of clients is extremely impressive (I'm looking forward to hearing how that company DFENS do; I shall definitely invest in some shares when they do go public) and he even has connections at the BBC.

I'm also looking forward to our next meeting. We'll be able to tackle the problem of correct reporting by junior staff. That will be a major achievement.

Best Regards
Jane
Project Manager

Malbury Centre Health Clinic

43 Green Lanes, Malbury, WS2 HH5

To: J Allbright
32 Pinetree Road
Malbury WS9 JG8
Reference Code : ALLBRIGHTJIM2003_0000000002

28th May 2003

1. Thank you for your letter concerning Glazing Maintenance Project, Reference KL/000001/AE/9/4.3.

2. Process of tender for contract phase II :

3. In order to evaluate your company's ability to carry out successfully and qualitatively the requirements of the relevant contract a Council auditor is required to assess the staff and equipment assigned to the contract. Consequently :

4. A Jenkins

5. will be attending your head office in connection with this requirement. An appointment for :

6. 10/06/2004 at 10:00

7. has been scheduled. If you cannot attend the appointment you must contact Malbury Council Project Services in writing before 05/06/2004. Please do not contact the Clinic directly, as appointment scheduling is carried out centrally for all departments.

8. As per your request I enclose Form ACC985, Claim For Expenses. You must return the form in the pre-paid envelope.

9. I have passed your comments on to our Auditing Department as required by Council rules. In order to comply with the Data Protection Act and European Union laws your name was not included in the communication, only the reference code.

10. Further enclosed is printout R76_20030303_ALLBRIGHT JIM2003_2_0000000005, a transcript of the information held within this communication for reference should any dispute arise. If you feel that the transcript does not truly reflect this communication you must query the matter with the Council Monitoring Department.

11. If you have any queries regarding this matter you must quote the reference above when contacting us.

S Goodwin

pp The Administrator

P.S.

Hiya Jim!

Funny how school seems so long ago yet like yesterday. I hardly see anyone I knew at school these days, but I'm sure they must be around somewhere. What I remember is spending the whole time trying to attract the boys, trying to impress your mates by drinking as much as you could, trying to stay out of trouble with the cops, and trying not to get pregnant. I see schoolgirls doing exactly the same things these days, but it's funny - they look so stupid, the boys look, well, unimpressive if you know what I mean (horrible, really) - and I suppose we looked just the same, but I don't remember it that way. Must be something about growing up.

I saw a boy I used to have a crush on when I was at school the other day. Course he's grown up now, but why on earth I had a crush on him I don't know - never had a good word to say about anything, every second word the f word, always criticising everything. I think we thought he was a bit of a rebel. Now he's older he still does the same, but it's mainly in a pub after a few pints - it isn't going to get him anywhere. And it seems that these days every first word is the f word, if that's possible. I reckon he'll still be complaining when he's seventy.

Thinking about it, none of us really had any ambitions. We didn't think about becoming anything - one of my friends wanted to become a hairdresser, but that was about it. I don't want Helen to grow up like that. She's got real brains, I want her to use them properly.

I think, in a strange way, I was lucky that my Dad died when he did. I know that sounds really nasty, but I don't mean it to be, I really loved my Dad. But I was at that age when I thought I knew bloody everything. Screaming rows with my Mum every day, that sort of thing. We lived on Lenspark Estate - we called it Leningrad estate because it felt like a war zone, grey concrete and burnt out cars. If everything had continued I would have gone the same way as the others, drinking, drugs, getting pregnant too early, that sort of thing.

And then Dad died. Heart attack. I don't know how to put it, almost start blubbing when I think about it, silly cow.

Anyway, to cut a long story short, as they say, Mum and me got close, not really close, but a bit like two enemies just too tired to carry on fighting. We'd lost someone we loved, and we didn't realise until too late how much we loved him. He had taken out a life assurance policy, we didn't even know about it - seemed like the last thing he would do. Mum always called him a no-good drunken Irishman, and I think he liked to play the Irishman part, boozing down the pub all the time, though it was actually his father, my grandad, who was Irish. But he was a good Dad to us, never raised his voice let alone his hand. Always had these marvellous stories he told us when we were kids, lovely stories they were. And when he died the policy paid out enough for Mum to move us out of the estate to our own little house, not much, but somewhere that felt like a home.

That's what I want for my little Helen. A Dad, someone who comes back from work or the pub and gives her a hug and a cuddle and makes her feel the world is a magical place.

I do go on don't I? When you get to know me you'll find I can rabbit on for ages. I hope you don't mind?

I had a word with Graham when we went to dinner about getting that BNP thing removed from your file - he said that only the people who made the software can do that. Well, actually, he said something like "haven't they told you that only the people who made the software can do that", which isn't the same. I'm sure he could do it if he wanted to. I even gave him the full fluttering eyelashes treatment, asked him please, pretty please, but that only seemed to irritate him. And I was wearing my special little black number, very low-cut, but that didn't seem to impress him much either. Didn't make for a very good dinner. He can act like a spoilt little boy sometimes.

Food was good mind.

So have you met anyone yet?

Yes, we must meet up sometime. At this rate we'll be old and grey before that happens.

Sandi

xxx

P.P.S. Helen wants to know who this man is I write to. She sends a kiss.

43 Green Lanes, Malbury, WS2 HH5

To: J Allbright

32 Pinetree Road

Malbury WS9 JG8

Reference Code : ALLBRIGHTJAMES2003_0000000002

29th May 2003

1. Thank you for your letter concerning Glazing Maintenance Project, Reference KL/000001/AE/9/4.3.

2. Process of tender for contract phase II : In order to evaluate your company's ability to carry out successfully and qualitatively the requirements of the relevant contract a Council auditor is required to assess the staff and equipment assigned to the contract. Consequently :

3. A Jenkins

4. will be attending your head office in connection with this requirement. An appointment for :

5. 10/06/2004 at 12:00

6. has been scheduled. If you cannot attend the appointment please contact Malbury Council Project Services in writing before

7. 05/06/2004.

8. Do not contact the Clinic directly, as appointment scheduling is carried out centrally for all departments.

9. As per your request I enclose a Claim For Expenses Form form.

10. Further enclosed is printout R76_2003 0303_ALLBRIGHT JAMES2003_ - 2_0000000005, a transcript of the kama sutra should any dispute arise. If you feel that the transcript does not have pictures you must query the matter with the Council nunnery.

11. Note that all correspondence must be addressed. Council policy does not permit the use of titles such as Mr or Ms, in order to avoid potential male chauvinist pig sexist bias.

12. If you have any queries regarding this matter please waggle your ears when contacting us.

V Grateley

V Grateley

Senior Administrator

P.S.

My Dear James

Many thanks for all your suggestions, you don't know how helpful they are. Unfortunately we're still stuck on a name. I like the idea of just a single initial, but Jane thinks it doesn't sound serious enough. Jane has organised a meeting with a market research consultancy - they're called HiHo, maybe you've heard of them? They have a very good reputation, and are quite expensive, but then you have to pay for quality, don't you?

I see your point about using a single colour. We will have to see what HiHo have to say. They're at the cutting edge of modern design. I must admit I would prefer just the lavender, but you can't afford to ignore market forces these days. There is no place for companies unwilling to move with the times. Malbury Council used to be quite stick-in-the-mud, but they have vastly improved their services since we came on board - and we have turned around their cost/quality ratio.

Definitely something to be proud of.

You are right about putting that silly note on record about the other company being run by the BNP. I don't know what I was thinking about at the time. It would have been enough that everybody knew, there was no need to put it on file. If he finds out the council could be sued. But I can't delete it; part of the specification for the system was that nothing could be altered except by the software company who built the system - we have very strong security regulations. I might have a quiet word with the chief systems analyst. Have to keep it quiet though.

And finally, brilliant news! The BBC have replied! Jane and I are going to a meeting with them next week. It's all very hush-hush, we haven't told anyone else yet, so we'll have to call in sick or something, taking a day off would be a little too obvious. I'm really excited!

Wish me luck

Yours Sincerely

Valerie

x

P.P.S.

I always think of you as a mature, married man. Strange that we're corresponding like this, and have never met. If you're wondering what I look like, some people have compared me with that film star, the one in "Breaking Gently". I'm sure they're exaggerating, of course.

If you ever have a spare moment and would like to meet up for a drink let me know. There's a very good wine bar near to the council offices.

Malbury Council Accounts Department

Malbury Council Centre, Park Road, Malbury, WS8 HT9

To: J Allbright

32 Pinetree Road

Malbury WS9 JG8

Reference Code : ALLBRIGHTJIM2003_0000000002

1st June 2003

1. Notification of payment: Details : General expenses payment, breakdown attached

2. Payee : Jim Allbright

3. Account details : As specified in breakdown

4. Date of payment : 31/05/2003

5. Amount : £923.34 (Nine hundred and twenty three pounds and thirty four pence)

6. Accruals : £None (None)

7. Accrual Basis : Monthly interest

8. Method of Payment : Electronic Transfer

9. Contest : If you wish to contest this payment you must contact Malbury Services Auditing Department. This Department is unable to enter into any correspondence with you over this matter.

10. Declaration : This payment has been automatically generated by our computer services. The amounts may not be muddified.

Malbury Council Accounts Department

To: J Allbright

32 Pinetree Road

Malbury,WS9 JG8

Reference Code : ALLBRIGHTJAMES2003_0000000002

1st June 2003

1. Notification of payment: Details : General expenses payment, breakdown attached

2. Payee : James Allbright

3. Account details : As specified in breakdown

4. Date of payment : 31/05/2003

5. Amount : £876.22 (Eight hundred and seventy xis pounds and twenty two pence)

6. Accruals : £None (None)

8. Accrual Basis : Monthly interest

9. Method of Payment : Electronic Transfer

10. Contest : If you wish to contest this payment you must contact Malbury Services Auditing Department. This Department is unable to enter into any correspondence with you over this matter.

11. Declaration : This payment has been automatically generated by our computer services. The amounts may not be muddified.

Malbury Council Accounts Department

To: The Administrator
Malbury Centre Health Clinic
43 Green Lanes
Malbury WS2 HH5

5th June 2003

Dear Sandi pp The Administrator

Thank you for your letter dated 28th May 2003. Unfortunately it looks like your scheduling system has been playing up again - the appointment is set for a year ahead, unless that's forward planning.

Enclosed please find the usual completed Claim For Expenses Form form in the standard sealed envelope.

Could you please send me another Claim For Expenses Form form? Do you do them in other colours? Pink would be a nice change. Maybe you have some stocks of lavender lying around.

Yours Faithfully

Jim Allbright

J Allbright
32 Pinetree Road
Malbury WS9 JG8

P.S.

Hello Sandi! (I'm feeling on top of the world for some reason. Probably haven't woken up and realised I'm still on planet earth yet.)

I have to say I never had an ambition to be a copper when I was a kid. Fireman, soldier, yes, but not a copper - if you can call it an "ambition" in the first place. I came from the sort of neighbourhood where coppers were at best useless, at worst they were your enemy. Mostly we used them for entertainment, starting fires or making hoax calls just to see how they'd react, sort of stupid thing I recognised when I became a copper myself; harmless, probably, but hardly an encouraging childhood. Best thing a kid can do in those circumstances is get out. In the old days you could go overseas, Australia, Canada or the States. These days you need a degree before they'll have you. Or something like that.

Have you ever thought of emigrating?

Funny thing : almost all the blokes I knew in the force had been in minor trouble with the law as kids. I suppose the ones who'd been in major trouble had a record and weren't allowed in. We had a pretty practical approach to the whole business. Though there were one or two who saw it as, how can I describe it? A moral choice, almost. The right thing to do. Protecting society. Strange thing is, they didn't tend to last long. In the end British coppering is about people, and people can be very strange, but they're still people at the end of the day. (We had some visits from the French coppers, they thought we were barmy, but I think they went away with new ideas. They're different over there.)

I know Lenspark Estate well. When I was a copper we never went there without back-up, and at least two of us at a time. I see they're planning on pulling it down. About time. Terrible place.

Your Dad sounds like a real character. He wasn't nicknamed "Sweets" was he? An old Sergeant used to reminisce about an Irishman called Sweets. Said he was the only decent bloke on the Estate. The sergeant had to nick him once for breaking and entering. He told me how Sweets had the court in tears, how he had only broken into the shop because he was drunk and in despair because it was his little daughter's birthday, and he wanted to take some sweets home for her, only the shop had shut early, and he would pay for the damage your honour, but could your honour please think of the wee children and how they would feel if their father was sent to jail for loving his little angel so much? The Sergeant had us in hysterics over that. Used to tell it as if he were Sweets, tears pouring down his cheeks. Apparently the judge himself was almost in tears at the end. Gave him a conditional discharge and slipped him a fiver afterwards to buy some sweets for the poor little girl. God, that was funny. The way the sergeant told it, anyhow. I've always wondered if it were true, and whether the Irish bloke was being serious. Kind of makes me wish my dad had been like that. Though there was never anything wrong with my dad, I hasten to add.

This Graham of yours sounds a bit dodgy. When did he last have a holiday?

There's a new barmaid at the local. Aussie. She's agreed to go to the Tate Modern with me next Sunday. I'll have to try keep clear of those funny exhibits. She might think I was a pervert.

Fancy a trip to the Tate some time? I promise we'll keep away from the funny section.

Tell Helen thanks for the kiss, and that I think she's a real sweety. Give her a kiss from me.

Jim

P.P.S.

Your Old Moo has been sending me letters. I've been winding her up something chronic. Feeling a little guilty about it. I think I shall have to put her off a little.

P.P.P.S

I was thinking the other day the council could have their own theme tune - "We'll bury you in the morning, ding dong the bells are going to chime, we'll bury you in paperwork" - or something like that (don't ever let me start singing, I'm terrible at it).

To: The Senior Administrator

Malbury Centre Health Clinic

43 Green Lanes

Malbury WS2 HH5

5th June 2003

Dear Senior Administrator Valerie Grateley

Thank you for your letter dated 28th May 2003. Unfortunately it looks like your scheduling system has been playing up again - the appointment is set for a year ahead, unless that's forward planning.

Enclosed please find the usual completed Claim For Expenses Form form in the standard sealed envelope.

Could you please send me another Claim For Expenses Form form?

Yours Faithfully

James Allbright

J Allbright

32 Pinetree Road

Malbury WS9 JG8

P.S.

Dear Val

I was thinking about the BBC programme, and wondering whether you shouldn't be a bit careful. Sometimes they can make people look silly, deliberately. Reading the reviews can be a little painful.

Maybe you want a simple company name. I haven't heard of this company HiHo, are you sure about them? You wouldn't want to be paying good money for buzz words. Some of these new marketing consultancies are, you could say, a bunch of cowboys. All glamour and glitz, no substance. Not that I want to put you off, mind, I just think you need to approach these things with a little care.

I would stick with just the lavender. Keep things simple.

Good luck

James

P.P.S.

Yes, happily married with ~~three~~ five children, all at university.

To: J Allbright

32 Pinetree Road

Malbury WS9 JG8

Reference Code : ALLBRIGHTJIM2003_0000000002

10th June 2003

1. Thank you for your letter concerning Glazing Maintenance Project, Reference KL/000001/AE/9/4.3.

2. Process of tender for contract phase II :

3. In order to evaluate your company's ability to carry out successfully and qualitatively the requirements of the relevant contract a Council auditor is required to assess the staff and equipment assigned to the contract. Consequently :

4. A Jenkins

5. will be attending your head office in connection with this requirement. An appointment for :

6. 20/06/2003 at 14:00

7. has been scheduled. If you cannot attend the appointment please contact Malbury Council Project Services in writing before 20/06/2003. Please do not contact the Clinic directly, as appointment scheduling is carried out centrally for all departments.

As per your request I enclose Form ACC985, Claim For Expenses. You must return the form in the pre-paid envelope.

8. I have passed your comments on to our Auditing Department as required by Council rules. In order to comply with the Data Protection Act and European Union laws your name was not included in the communication, only the reference code.

9. Further enclosed is printout R76_20030303_ALLBRIGHT JIM2003_2_0000000006, a transcript of the information held within this communication for reference should any dispute arise. If you feel that the transcript does not truly reflect this communication you must query the matter with the Council Monitoring Department.

10. If you have any queries regarding this matter you must quote the reference above when contacting us.

S Goodwin

pp The Administrator

P.S.

Jim, my spiritual soul mate and fellow rebel against the system!

(Okay, I admit it, I nicked that out of a book the Old Moo left lying around, but it does sound good, doesn't it? And she probably thinks a rebel is some sort of special tea-towel from one of those expensive shops in London. If she knows what a tea-towel is. Am I being too bitchy?)

Sorry about mucking up the appointment. Damn computer system again! There are so many things you have to remember - there's one section where you have to enter a 'Y' for 'yes', only if you don't enter it in lower case, like 'y', it thinks you're entering an 'n', or not a 'Y', if you see what I mean (not sure I do myself). Everywhere else it automatically changes that sort of thing into upper case. And the software company say that, because it was signed off - they council have to sign that they've accepted it - it's the council's mistake. They're prepared to correct it if the council pay them - something like fifteen grand! Fifteen grand to fix a mistake you made yourself in the first place!

I think I should become a computer programmer or whatever they're called.

Yes! Sweets! That was my Dad. I knew he was called Sweets down at his local, but what you said about him breaking into a shop, I reckon that was when I was five. I only vaguely remembered something about that, Mum having a real go at him on my birthday, but I never really knew what it was about, I was just upset because I wanted a birthday party and Mum said we couldn't afford one. Bless him! I'm sure the silly sod did break in to bring home some sweets for me, he was a real softy, especially when he'd had a few. He didn't earn a lot, and he spent too much of it on the booze. I think he had what they call a guilt complex about it. Just makes me love him all the more. He used to call me and my sister his little angels.

I remember him saying one day, after I had had yet another argument with my Mum, not long after I'd turned sixteen, he said something about taking it easy on Mum, and then something about, not to worry so much, when he was gone, there'd be an angel in heaven looking over me. I thought he was just pissed again as usual, but now I think he knew he was going to die soon. He always said he was fey, but I thought it was his pretending to be more Irish than the Irish.

At the funeral the priest gave a sermon, what do you call it, a eulogy? Another new word I learnt then. And I learnt how my own Dad, the father I had, well, ignored, was loved by the community - as the priest said - and me and Mum found out how much we had loved him, and how little we had known it.

Damn! I'm starting to blubber like a kid. I must stop this nonsense or Helen will get upset. Stupid cow.

Right. Hope the paper dries before you get this.

Anyway.

My sister married an Aussie. Went off to Australia five years ago. I hardly hear from her these days - never seem to get a chance to write, and I can't afford to phone her very often, just around Christmas usually, from the public call box, if it's working. Mum's always going on about what a success she's made of her life, how they're planning on buying a house with a swimming pool, that sort of thing. As if somehow I'm a total loser, you know, single mum, no husband. She's very old-fashioned - Mum, that is. I don't go around to see her very often, can't stand the snide remarks. Anyway, she lives in Dornton now, and it costs a fortune to get there.

Peggy - that's my sister - said I should get a computer so we could stay in touch with email. Easy enough for her to say, those things are expensive, and it would mean getting a phone in and that costs money I can't afford, or rather money I need for Helen. I can't use the computer at work, they've set it up so we can't send emails outside, and it's a sackable offence to receive personal stuff. I mean, how can they blame us if someone else sends us an email?

Bloody 21st century, marvels of technology, all that stuff, and they do their best to make sure we can't use it.

Graham said he would get me a cheap second hand computer, but I haven't seen him since the dinner, so I guess he's pissed off with me for some reason. I mean, it's not like we're going out or anything.

Talking of going out just makes me depressed. Why is it there are so many men out there and I can't find one? Maybe Mum's right.

So how was the date with the Aussie? And when are you coming round here so that I can see you? I'd love to go to the Tate with you, but the neighbour's away most weekends, and I can't take Helen with us, if they let kids in anyway.

Helen says thank you very much, and she's sure she likes you a lot. She sends you three kisses. That means you're special. Very special.

Sandi

xxx

P.P.S. Go on, wind the Old Moo up. She deserves it.

To: J Allbright

32 Pinetree Road

Malbury

WS9 JG8

Reference Code : ALLBRIGHTJAMES2003_0000000002

11th June 2003

1. Thank you for your letter concerning Glazing Maintenance Project, Reference KL/000001/AE/9/4.3.

2. Process of tender for contract phase II :

3. In order to evaluate your company's ability to carry out successfully and qualitatively the requirements of the relevant contract a Council auditor is required to assess the staff and equipment assigned to the contract. Consequently :

4. A Jenkins

5. will be attending your head office in connection with this requirement. An appointment for :

6. 20/06/2003 at 15:00

7. has been scheduled. If you cannot attend the appointment please contact Malbury Council Project Services in writing before 20/06/2003. Do not contact the Clinic directly, as appointment scheduling is carried out centrally for all departments.

8. As per your request I enclose Form ACC985, Claim For Expenses. You must return the form in the pre-paid envelope.

9. Further enclosed is printout R76_20030303_ ALLBRIGHTJAMES2003_- 2_0000000006, a transcript of the current dispute. Arise. If you feel that the transcript does not you must query the matter with the Council hickory dickory dock.

10. Note that all correspondence must be addressed. Council policy does not permit the use of titles such as Mr or Ms, in order to avoid potential road kill slaughter gender bias delete as applicable.

11. If you have any queries regarding this matter you must contact the auditors.

V Grateley

V Grateley
Senior Administrator

P.S.

My Dear James

Sincere apologies for the mistake in the date. It must make us look horribly unprofessional, which is something I really cannot stand. Unfortunately with a computer system of the size of ours we have to expect a few small glitches here and there - though we did our absolute best to minimise any problems. I've scheduled another appointment for you, but you will need to write to Project Services to have the other one cancelled; unfortunately I can't do it from here. It was part of the design of the system, to prevent junior staff from abusing the system. Really I should be able to make my own modifications, being a Senior Administrator. I shall get that resolved as soon as possible.

I know what you mean, about certain television programmes demeaning the people who appear on them, but this is different; Jane and I are professionals, we're not some silly couple begging someone to repair the DIY they couldn't finish, or anything of that nature. In fact the programme could turn out to be a standard reference for people planning on starting their own companies; we've insisted on a clause in the contract with the BBC whereby we will receive royalties for every copy sold.

In fact they're going to start filming pretty soon - it's certainly exciting. I'm really looking forward to it. So much to do before then - I'll need a new outfit, hairdo, we have to get Jane's spare room looking like an office. Hundreds of little things to take care of!

I've checked up on HiHo - I agree that we have to be careful, but their references are impeccable. Most come from the United States; they have only just opened their branch in England a couple of months ago, but the American way is definitely the way of the future. Admittedly the names of the American companies they have worked with - "Al's Motor Spares" was one - sound silly to us, but they do things differently over there. I'm told the motor spares company is going to go nation-wide soon. I think it's something to do with cars.

We have compiled a list of possible company names; it will be part of the first "shoot" as the television people call it. Jane and I deciding on a name, with Vince Spiro from HiHo providing valuable input. At the same time we will decide on company colours, all the things that define what our company will be. We definitely need a mission statement, a company ethos. And a website. And a marketing strategy.

So many things to think about! Please let me know if you have any suggestions. A helping hand from an experienced entrepreneur such as yourself never goes amiss.

Yours Fondly

Valerie Grateley

xx

P.P.S. Five children all at university! You must be proud of them. I don't see myself ever having children, not as a professional with a career - unless I meet someone of similar thought prepared to pay for nannies to look after the dear things while I'm working. I'm sure your wife must be proud of having a husband like yourself. I expect she feels the strain of having five children.

Malbury Council Centre, Park Road, Malbury, WS8 HT9

Reference Code : ALLBRIGHTJIM2003_0000000002

23rd June 2003

To : S Goodwin

Audit Report

1. Auditor : A Jenkins
2. Details : Company audit to ensure compliance with council requirements
3. Company : Jim Allbright
4. Contact : Jim Allbright
5. Outcome : [Pass/Fail] Pass
6. Free Text :

I can without hesitation recommend Mr Allbright's tender for contract. Not only does he have three buckets where one would suffice, he also has two squeegees, and is planning on buying a brand new one for larger windows. And he has three ladders. And four cloths, two of which are almost new. And an almost full bottle of window cleaning liquid.

I would query whether this idea of auditing every single possible job contract the council has going is perhaps just a little counter-productive - the cleaning of a clinic window hardly involves national security, after all - but I have no wish to have to sit through the explanations I heard the last time, none of which made sense and all of which gave me a headache.

But at least I now know that the Dog and Duck down Emery Lane does a really tasty pie and chips. I believe their Chicken-in-a-basket also comes recommended. It will make a nice walk on Fridays when I'm retired, which fortunately is only a few years away.

Oh, and Mr Allbright wanted me to note in this report that he was wearing a clean shirt, newly ironed, and very good it looked too. I can also confirm that he has no grey hairs or bad habits. He is indeed the epitome of an eligible bachelor, with a sense of humour no independent young woman could resist.

Signed :

Alan Jenkins

MALBURY COUNCIL AUDIT DEPARTMENT

Malbury Council Centre, Park Road, Malbury, WS8 HT9

Reference Code : ALLBRIGHTJAMES2003_0000000002

23rd June 2003

To : V Grateley

Audit Report

1. Auditor : A Jenkins
2. Details : Company audit to ensure compliance with council requirements
3. Company : Jim Allbright
4. Contact : Jim Allbright
5. Outcome : [Pass/Fail] Pass
6. Free Text :

And passed with flying colours, may I say. In all the audits I have been commissioned to undertake I can say without doubt that Mr Allbright's has been the most fascinating I have ever done. I have audited major corporations for compliance with Malbury's exacting standards, but never before has there been such a spirit of co-operation and open access to facilities and staff. Amongst some points to highlight : staff have full access to hygiene and refreshment facilities via an inter-company exchange agreement with the Dog and Duck establishment. A full flexi-time operation is an integral part of company policy. Safety is ensured by means of specialised and high-tech rubber attachments to all ladders. All equipment is backed up by replacement units on-site, and a commercial agreement with the community-based company Naidoo's Local Supermarket supplies extra technical requirements should the backups fail. He is further planning a major financial investment to modernise existing hardware.

I can easily recommend Mr Allbright's tender for contract.

However there is one point which I was not able to respond to, and which I hereby pass on for further elucidation : Mr Allbright was concerned that his equipment was sourced from acceptable sources - acceptable, that is, to Malbury Council's new, innovative and eclectic standards - and he is aware that one of his buckets has "Made in China" stamped on it. I'm afraid I am unaware of whether or not Malbury Council regard China as an acceptable source. I have informed Mr Allbright that I have full confidence in Malbury Council's ability to establish a quorum, a committee, indeed a think-group, to hammer out this most complex and important issue.

Which reminds me of another issue which arose during the compliance audit: can someone send me a Claim For Expenses Form form?

Signed :

Alan Jenkins

Malbury Council Accounts Department

Malbury Council Centre, Park Road, Malbury, WS8 HT9

To: J Allbright

32 Pinetree Road

Malbury WS9 JG8

Ref. : ALLBRIGHTJIM2003_0000000002

1st July 2003

1. Notification of payment

2. Details : General expenses payment, breakdown attached

3. Payee : Jim Allbright

4. Account details : As specified in breakdown

5. Date of payment : 30/06/2003

6. Amount : £872.66 (Eight hundred and seventy-two punds and xisty-xis pence)

7. Accruals : £None (None)

8. Accrual Basis : Monthly interest

9. Method of Payment : Electronic Transfer

10. Contest : If you wish to contest this payment you must contact Malbury Services Auditing Department. This Department is unable to enter into any correspondence with you over this matter.

11. Declaration : This payment has been automatically generated by our computer services. The amounts may not be muddified.

Malbury Council Accounts Department

Malbury Council Accounts Department

Malbury Council Centre, Park Road, Malbury, WS8 HT9

To: J Allbright

32 Pinetree Road

Malbury WS9 JG8

Ref. Code : ALLBRIGHTJAMES2003_0000000002

1st July 2003

1. Notification of payment

2. Details : General expenses payment, breakdown attached

3. Payee : James Allbright

4. Account details : As specified in brakedown

5. Date of payment : 30/06/2003

6. Amount : £902.54 (Nine hundred and two pounds and fifty-four pence)

7. Accruals : £Nun (None)

8. Accrual Basis : Monthly interest

9. Method of Payment : Eclectic Transfer

10. Contest : If you wish to contest this payment you must contact Malbury Services Auditioning Department. This Department is unable to enter into any correspondence with you over this matter.

11. Declaration : This payment has been automatically aerated by our computer sufferers. The amounts may not be muddified.

Malbury Council Accounts Department

To: Malbury Centre Health Clinic
43 Green Lanes
Malbury WS2 HH5

12th July 2003

Dear Sandi pp The Administrator

Thank you for your letter dated 10th June 2003.

Enclosed please find the usual completed Claim For Expenses Form form in the standard sealed envelope.

Could you please send me another Claim For Expenses Form form?

Yours Faithfully

Jim Allbright

J Allbright
32 Pinetree Road
Malbury
WS9 JG8

P.S. Dear Sandi

Apologies for taking so long to reply. You remember asking about Kayley, that Aussie barmaid? Well, we did go to the Tate, and had a great time - she insisted on seeing the dodgy exhibits, killed herself laughing at them, she really does have a down to earth Australian sense of humour (and quite a filthy one sometimes) - and a few days later we went out to some movie or other, one of those action ones, very enjoyable, totally forgettable - can't even remember the name of it, but had a good time.

Anyway, when Alan turned up for the audit - Alan Jenkins - we had a good laugh about him having to count the same buckets twice, once for James and once for Jim, and then went down the local for a late lunch. He left after a couple of hours, but I stayed on because Kayley was starting at seven in the evening, and I decided I may as well wait to say Hi seeing as I was there anyway. There was this other bloke there, looked all of about sixteen, and acted about twelve. Drunk as a lord. Made rude remarks about Kayley's figure when she turned up and kept on making them. So I told him to shut it, and he got shirty, and we had what I believe is called a full and frank exchange of opinions. About three broken tables and five broken barstools worth of full and frank exchange.

Now that might sound bad, but that's not what happened. Okay, he tried to punch me, but he was so drunk he was wasting his time. I admit I had maybe had more than usual, which is why I tripped as I stepped backwards, intending to let him fall on his face. Unfortunately I fell on one of the tables, which promptly broke. Pete - the landlord - has had the furniture for so long it's falling to pieces. The other bloke fell over sideways and took out another table. At the time I was busy coming to terms with various pieces of broken table, but I could have sworn I saw Pete nip out from behind the bar to break the third table. He's claiming it on the insurance; can't claim for wear and tear, but he can claim for brand new ones if it's an accident. Some bloody accident.

As for the bar stools, they were in Pete's storeroom at the time. They fell apart months ago; the only thing keeping them together was woodworm, and that died. Pete just brought them in for the cops to see so he could add them to the insurance claim.

When the cops turned up they weren't in a mood for polite chatter. The young bloke and I got chucked straight into the back of a van, down the nick, and into separate cells. I tried explaining that I was an ex-copper and innocent, but they weren't listening. Coppers these days just aren't trained properly. It was okay for the kid - he'd passed out when he fell over the table and hadn't come to. Anyway, to cut a long story short, they only released us in the morning. I must have clipped my head because it hurt like hell when I woke up. And my arm was aching. One of the coppers was too enthusiastic with his arm-lock, especially seeing as how it wasn't even necessary. The kid was worse off though; apart from looking terrible, his missus had come to fetch him - obviously married young, the pair of them didn't seem over eighteen, but she had the look of someone for whom this had happened once too often. I almost felt sorry for him. I wouldn't like to have her greeting me in the morning when if I had a hangover and I'd done something wrong.

Then again, I could more or less see her point of view, if you know what I mean.

I had to go down to the nick three or four times following that, to "give a statement", which is just their way of making life difficult for people they can't charge. (I might have accidentally nudged the one in the ribs at the pub, I seem to vaguely remember something like that, but they had no right to nick me.) Pete and Kayley had both said that it was just an accident after a bit of ribbing, so the cops couldn't really do anything about it. Got a real earful from Kayley, though. About how she could handle herself, Pete would have thrown the little sod out himself, and she didn't need the interference from some drunken yob, etc, etc, et-bloody-cetera. The ex-wife used to do that as well. I mean, it wasn't as if I was actually drunk. Not really. Not legless like the kid. So I decided to give the pub a miss for a while and go to the Nelson instead. And I've had to put extra effort in to get rid of the backlog of jobs caused by spending time with the audit man, and the days down the local nick, and the arm being out of action for a while.

How's the computer system going?

Jim

P.P.S.

I did think of trying your Dad's trick, but somehow I didn't think I could pull it off - somehow I think the sight of me weeping before a judge I reckon would get me an extra six months - if it came to that, of course.

P.P.P.S. What sort of sweets does Helen like?

To: The Senior Administrator
Malbury Centre Health Clinic
43 Green Lanes
Malbury WS2 HH5

12th July 2003

Dear Senior Administrator Valerie Grateley

Thank you for your letter dated 11th June 2003.

Enclosed please find the usual completed Claim For Expenses Form form in the standard sealed envelope.

Could you please send me another Claim For Expenses Form form?

Yours Faithfully

James Allbright

J Allbright
32 Pinetree Road
Malbury WS9 JG8

P.S.

Dear Valerie

Apologies for taking so long to reply, but I've been rushed off my feet due to staff absenteeism. Apparently there's something going around.

How's the television programme going?

Good luck

James

Malbury Centre Health Clinic

43 Green Lanes, Malbury, WS2 HH5

To: J Allbright

32 Pinetree Road

Malbury WS9 JG8

Reference Code : ALLBRIGHTJIM2003_0000000002

16th July 2003

1. Thank you for your letter concerning Glazing Maintenance Project, Reference KL/000001/AE/9/4.3.

2. As per your request I enclose Form ACC985, Claim For Expenses. You must return the form in the pre-paid envelope.

3. I have passed your comments on to our Auditing Department as required by Council rules. In order to comply with the Data Protection Act and European Union laws your name was not included in the communication, only the reference code.

4. Further enclosed is printout R76_20030303_ALLBRIGHT JIM2003_2_0000000007, a transcript of the information held within this communication for reference should any dispute arise. If you feel that the transcript does not truly reflect this communication you must query the matter with the Council Monitoring Department.

5. If you have any queries regarding this matter you must quote the reference above when contacting us.

S Goodwin

pp The Administrator

P.S.

Hey, Jim, how's it going! Recovered yet?

Sorry to hear about your troubles. I hope that horrible little scroat gets all he deserves from his wife. She should hit him with a frying pan. Several times preferably. And I think that Kayley sounds a bit stuck up. I mean, you were just trying to protect her, after all. She should be thankful that a bloke was ready to do the right thing. But that's Aussie girls for you. I think they're all raving feminists. You're better off without her, she doesn't sound like your type.

The computer system is about as normal as it ever is, which is to say useless. Part of it is an automatic re-ordering system. Before they installed it the various departments would have a stock take once a month and order according to what they thought they would need the next month. Now the system does the calculations. Which is why they've had to rent a storeroom to hold an extra fifty boxes of paper towels, but are short on disinfectant for public toilets. I don't understand exactly how it works - Graham did explain it to me, but most of it went over my head. Apparently they use an "algorythm" which works on historical data, only because the system's so new it didn't have enough data, so it threw a wobbly. Problem is that it's automatic, so no-one can stop it.

I did have a chuckle when it ordered fourteen beds to the main Council office. How it worked out that a Council office needs fourteen beds I don't know. But I do know they disappeared pretty quickly, and I don't think they were sent back, if you know what I mean.

I could do with a new bed myself, but I don't think I'm likely to be able to snaffle one like they did.

It's nice to be able to have a chuckle. This job can get pretty depressing sometimes. The only reason I stick it is because they pay Helen's kindergarten fees. Dad used to tell me I was a lucky one - my sister had the brains, and I had the luck. If he could see me now he'd probably think again. Feels like the only luck in my life is my little Helen, and I can't even give her the father she needs.

Sorry if I sound a bit down. I promise it doesn't happen often.

Graham remembered the computer he promised. He said it's an old one, though it looks quite new. When I asked how much it cost he said it was a present, which is really nice of him. Maybe he was feeling a bit sorry about being offish.

He installed it and put everything together in the lounge - I only have a small flat, so there wasn't anywhere else. Had to get a telephone line installed, but he'd gone through all the pricing stuff and found me something affordable (hope so, cause if it's the telephone or decent clothes for Helen, the telephone goes). All those cables, though! Still, it's working like a dream, I can get onto the Internet and everything! Even have my own email address, so my sis in Australia can send me news, that is if they aren't too busy sunning themselves around their swimming pool. (No, honestly, if they have a swimming pool, good luck to them.)

Helen thinks Graham is wonderful. Keeps asking when "Uncle Graham" is coming around again. And Graham has taken a fancy to her too. Never thought of him as the kind of bloke who's happy around kids, but he was very patient with all her questions. And he taught her not to play with any of the cables - if I told her not to do that she'd be pulling everything out the minute my back was turned. Why is it kids are always at war with their mothers, and yet sweet as innocents when some stranger turns up? No, I didn't mean that, she's normally as good as gold, my little angel.

Got the audit report back from Alan - he's a great bloke, lovely sense of humour. I almost wet myself when I read what he'd written. He really took the mick out of the council rules. Lucky bugger is going to retire soon. Wish I could do that myself. He gave you what they call a "glowing recommendation", so with any luck you should get the job soon. I can't believe it's taken this long just to get a window cleaned!

Hope you're fully recovered from the battle. And hope to see you soon. That's soon, as in Very Soon!!!

Love
Sandi
xxx

Malbury Centre Health Clinic Senior Administrators' Department

43 Green Lanes, Malbury, WS2 HH5

To: J Allbright

32 Pinetree Road

Malbury WS9 JG8

Reference Code : ALLBRIGHTJAMES2003_0000000002

17th July 2003

1. Thank you for your letter concerning Glazing Maintenance Project, Reference KL/000001/AE/9/4.3.

2. As per your request I enclose Form ACC985, Claim For Expenses. You must return the form in the pre-paid envelope.

3. Further enclosed is printout R76_20030303_ ALLBRIGHTJAMES2003_- 2_0000000007, a transcript of the current dispute. Arise. If you feel that the transcript does not you must query the matter with the Council Maternity Services.

4. Note that all correspondence must be addressed. Council policy does not permit the use of titles such as Mr or Ms, in order to avoid.

5. If you have any queries regarding this matter please contact the auditors.

V Grateley

V Grateley

Senior Administrator

P.S.

My Dear James

I know what you mean about staff absenteeism. Councils traditionally suffer from a high rate of lower ranked employees 'throwing a sickie', as I believe the phrase is. Here at Malbury we in senior management have put a tremendous effort in to reduce such unnecessary absences, including incentives such as home visits to reassure the staff that the Council has their welfare at heart. We've also instituted awards and signed recommendations for staff with the least number of days off 'ill'. But it is an uphill struggle. I'm afraid there is an institutional culture in this country which sees such things as being a perk of the job. I blame the unions, personally.

The television programme is proceeding extremely well. The director (John Harlow) and producer (Maggie Simkins) - I'm not too sure what each is supposed to do, but they are really professional - are very supportive, and have given us all sorts of advice on how to maximise our image. Not that Jane and I need much advice, of course. I think we represent what I like to call the "modern professional woman".

The scriptwriters - what they need scriptwriters for I don't know - and the camera crew and other support staff are not what I would call professional, I'm afraid. We had to reshoot a few scenes quite a few times because they were laughing at some joke or other. Honestly, telling jokes while they're supposed to be filming! I'm surprised the director and producer (whoever it is that hires them) hasn't fired them. But I hear the BBC have their own problems with unions.

And we've chosen a name at last! Vince was a great help - he's very comfortable in front of the cameras, I suppose in his work he has to be. We went through a whole list we had compiled - "J & V", "The ConsultantZ", "Cons R Us" (Con for consultant), "Systems Solutions" (I like that one, but apparently the initials aren't user-friendly), "ConTemp" (for contemporary, to suggest modernity and up-to-dateness). There were some based on the theme of "Project", but Vince explained how research has shown that companies with a small "j" in their name are hardly ever big players in the internationalised global market. In the end we settled on C-Girls, short for

Consultant Girls. Of course we can't employ only women, but Jane and I will be the main players, and it gives a positive image of a modern, forward-looking company.

Yours Sincerely

Valerie Grateley

xx

P.P.S. Received the Audit Report. Looks very good. I'm sure you'll be awarded the contract. I'm meeting Sir Henry Walters tomorrow, and will put in a good word.

To: The Administrator
Malbury Centre Health Clinic
43 Green Lanes
Malbury WS2 HH5

20th July 2003

Dear Sandi pp The Administrator

Thank you for your letter dated 10th June 2003.

Enclosed please find the usual completed Claim For Expenses Form form in the standard sealed envelope.

Could you please send me another Claim For Expenses Form form?

Yours Faithfully

Jim Allbright

J Allbright
32 Pinetree Road
Malbury, WS9 JG8

P.S.

Dear Sandi

Yes, all fully recovered and back in fighting trim. And Kayley phoned up to ask where I had been, and whether I'd been avoiding her. Silly thing to suggest. I explained how I'd been more than busy of late, and the long and short of it is that we're apparently going out together again, I think.

But if another bloke starts making comments about her she can thump him herself.

I don't understand this computer system of yours. The one at the council, that is. I mean, I understand it's got these problems but why doesn't someone do anything about them? Not that I know much about computers; as a beat bobby you don't get to use them much. I was thinking of getting a PC to see what the fuss is about the internet, but it's a lot of money for something you might not use much. Can't see myself getting into these chat rooms. If you believe what you read in the papers they're full of twelve year-olds and perverts trying to pick up the twelve year-olds - or is it the twelve year-olds who are the perverts?. Let me know if you find yours useful, I might think about getting a cheap second hand machine somewhere.

Just realised, re-reading that paragraph, that "PC" could mean Police Constable. Reads a little funny that way. I meant personal computer, just in case there's any misunderstanding.

I envy blokes like Graham who can get on with kids. But I suppose when you're in uniform you become the enemy - the face of authority, as they call it - you get respect if you're firm, but they don't come out to hug you.

I don't know if you've considered it, but you don't suppose he fancies you? The computer and the rest of it might be his way of saying so. Just a thought.

Alan certainly has a good sense of humour. He said you have to, working for the council. He reckoned that the council was always inefficient, but inefficient in a human way. There were always shortcuts to getting things done, phoning someone you knew in another department to get things moving, that sort of thing. Now that it's all organised and computerised and projecturised (his word) things take fifteen times as long, if they ever get done at all. He thinks there's a hole in the computer system where things get lost. Not sure if that's possible, though. I thought computers remembered every little thing, just like the wife used to.

I'm sure your Dad was right about you being lucky, even if sometimes it doesn't feel that way. I'm pretty good at knowing when someone's a lucky person, and I can feel it in your letters. And you remember that one time I saw you, when you were chatting to the receptionist in the clinic? The first thought that came into my head was, now there's a lucky girl, definitely.

One good thing about the little fracas in the pub; Pete gave me the first drink free when I went back there. Reckons he'd been waiting ages for a punch-up so that he could claim on the furniture. Now he's got three brand new tables and a brand new set of barstools. Trouble is he still has another five tables he wants replacing. It won't be me giving him the excuse.

In a funny sort of a way I'll be a little sad when they decide on awarding the contract. It's been kind of fun watching the strange workings of the system, and getting paid for writing letters.

But it will be nice to meet you at last. You and Helen, of course.

At least three kisses for Helen. One day I'll be there to give them in person.

Jim

To: The Senior Administrator
Malbury Centre Health Clinic
43 Green Lanes
Malbury WS2 HH5

20th July 2003

Dear Senior Administrator Valerie Grateley

Thank you for your letter dated 11th June 2003.

Enclosed please find the usual completed Claim For Expenses Form form in the standard sealed envelope.

Could you please send me another Claim For Expenses Form form?

Yours Faithfully

James Allbright

J Allbright
32 Pinetree Road
Malbury
WS9 JG8

P.S.

Dear Val

Good to hear the programme's going well. I can relate to your feelings about unions, definitely wouldn't allow one in my company, they might try to take over. As far as staff making jokes while working, I'm afraid you'll never avoid that. At least it shows morale is high.

Interesting choice of name, C-Girls. I think it will definitely stick. In people's minds, that is. I shall keep an eye out for the programme - any idea when it's scheduled to appear?

Many thanks for putting a word in with Sir Henry Waters. If you ever need windows cleaned at a discount, let me know.

Good luck

James

Malbury Centre Health Clinic

43 Green Lanes, Malbury, WS2 HH5

To: J Allbright

32 Pinetree Road

Malbury WS9 JG8

Reference Code : ALLBRIGHTJIM2003_0000000002

25th July 2003

1. Thank you for your letter concerning Glazing Maintenance Project, Reference KL/000001/AE/9/4.3.

2. The tendering process has now been completed. I have to inform you that your bid was not successful.

3. As per your request I enclose Form ACC985, Claim For Expenses. You must return the form in the pre-paid envelope.

4. I have passed your comments on to our Auditing Department as required by Council rules. In order to comply with the Data Protection Act and European Union laws your name was not included in the communication, only the reference code.

5. Further enclosed is printout R76_20030303_ALLBRIGHT JIM2003_2_0000000008, a transcript of the information held within this communication for reference should any dispute arise. If you feel that the transcript does not truly reflect this communication you must query the matter with the Council Monitoring Department.

6. If you have any queries regarding this matter you must quote the reference above when contacting us.

S Goodwin

pp The Administrator

P.S.

Yo, Jim!

Bummer! Sorry about that, I was sure you were going to get the contract. I'll bet The Moo had something to do with it. She's been going around like the cat that got the cream as well. Something about a new company she's starting. God knows what sort of company. A boutique, no doubt. Selling fancy clothes to her posh friends. Stuck up old cow.

Even worse, Graham's in trouble with that lot now. The senior managers, as they call themselves. They reckon he's been fiddling with the system, making it print rude comments, that sort of thing. He doesn't seem worried, but I am. He could lose his job, and with that on your record he'd never get another one in computers. He says I shouldn't worry, because everyone's been told that only the company that makes the software can change anything. He doesn't know what they're like, though. They could believe that two plus two made twenty-seven if they wanted to.

I don't think he fancies me, not as anything more than a friend. He'd have said something by now. Sometimes I wonder if he isn't gay. Not in not fancying me, just he doesn't have a girlfriend, so you get to wonder. Doesn't make any difference if he is, of course, he's a good mate and I worry about him.

You liar! I bet the first thing that popped into your head when you saw me was the first thing that pops into all blokes' heads when they see a woman they don't know. I know what you men are like! But thanks for saying what you said, it was sweet of you. Sometimes I feel as if Dad were watching over me somehow - the only problem is he keeps nipping off to that pub in the sky just when I need him most.

And don't believe that nonsense about kids respecting you but not liking you. When you get to meet Helen I'm sure you'll fall in love with her, and she'll think you're the bees knees.

Good to hear you're back together with Kayley. If you like her she can't be that bad.

Feels like I'll never get to meet you the way things are going. Unless you fancy a drink one Friday after work? I can give Graham some excuse, he won't mind. He knows I'm looking for someone.

Sandi

xxx

PPS

Helen sends three kisses to you.

43 Green Lanes, Malbury, WS2 HH5

To: J Allbright

32 Pinetree Road

Malbury WS9 JG8

Reference Code : ALLBRIGHTJAMES2003_0000000002

25th July 2003

1. Thank you for your letter concerning Glazing Maintenance Project, Reference KL/000001/AE/9/4.3.

2. The tendering process has been completed. I have to inform you that your bid has been accepted. Enclosed please find Forms TOC7623 and Contract of Signature TOC7622 with related pre-paid envelopes. Please return these in the envelopes provided.

3. As per your request I enclose Form ACC985, Claim For Expenses. You must return the form in the pre-paid envelope.

4. Further enclosed is printout R76_20030303_ ALLBRIGHTJAMES2003_- 2_0000000008, a transcript of the information held within this communication for reference should any dispute arise. If you feel that the transcript does not truly reflect this communication you must query the matter with the Council Monitoring Department.

5. If you have any queries regarding this matter you must quote the reference above when contacting us.

V Grateley

V Grateley

Senior Administrator

P.S.

My Dear James

Will have to make this short as we are amazingly busy at the moment. The television production is going ahead at full speed. Latest shoots - technical word they use in television - were Jane and I choosing the company colours, mission statement, location of office, right down to wallpaper design. You have to get everything precisely right, even the smallest points - especially the smallest points. Speaking of the office, we have chosen Maudley Street - you must know it, one of the more expensive areas, but image is everything. Can't operate out of a spare room as an office, now can we, not if we want to go as far as we want to.

They say the programme is scheduled for 'some time in August, maybe September'. You would have thought that the BBC could be a bit more organised. But apparently it means re-arranging some shows to fit our programme in. They obviously think it will be high profile. But that means that Jane and I will have to have the company operational by then. No good having all this expensive advertising and no way of taking the calls which will pour in afterwards. We're busy creating a schedule - when to have the office ready, when to advise the Council that we will, sadly, be leaving their employment for pastures new, all the hundred and one things.

Just think, in a month or so we will be celebrities!

Yours Sincerely

Valerie Grateley, C-Girl!

xx

P.P.S. I knew I could swing the contract your way. Had to do a bit of networking, but Sir Henry was most impressed with my work.

Malbury Council Accounts Department

Malbury Council Centre, Park Road, Malbury, WS8 HT9

To: J Allbright

32 Pinetree Road

Malbury WS9 JG8

Reference Code : ALLBRIGHTJIM2003_0000000002

1st August 2003

1. Notification of payment

Details : General expenses payment, breakdown attached

2. Payee : Jim Allbright

3. Account details : As specified in breakdown

4. Date of payment : 31/07/2003

5. Amount : £520.54 (Five hundred and twenty punds and fifty-four pence)

6. Accruals : £None (None)

7. Accrual Basis : Monthly interest

8. Method of Payment : Electronic Transfer

9. Contest : If you wish to contest this payment you must contact Malbury Services Auditing Department. This Department is unable to enter into any correspondence with you over this matter.

10. Declaration : This payment has been automatically generated by our computer services. The amounts may not be muddified.

Malbury Council Accounts Department

Malbury Council Accounts Department

Malbury Council Centre, Park Road, Malbury, WS8 HT9

To: J Allbright

32 Pinetree Road

Malbury WS9 JG8

Reference Code : ALLBRIGHTJAMES2003_0000000002

1st August 2003

1. Notification of payment

Details : General expenses payment, breakdown attached

2. Payee : James Allbright

3. Account details : As specified in breakdown

4. Date of payment : 31/07/2003

5. Amount : £632.23 (Six hundred and thirty-two punds and twenty-three pence)

6. Accruals : £None (None)

7. Accrual Basis : Monthly interest

8. Method of Payment : Electronic Transfer

9. Contest : If you wish to contest this payment you must contact Malbury Services Auditing Department. This Department is unable to enter into any correspondence with you over this matter.

10. Declaration : This payment has been automatically generated by our computer services. The amounts may not be muddified.

Malbury Council Accounts Department

Malbury Council Project Services

Internal E-Mail

Private And Confidential

From : J C Thornton

To : All Council Staff

cc : Peter V Hamilton

Sent : 11:22:31 1st August 2003

It has come to our attention that the council-wide system that we put into place several months back has been abused by certain members of staff. This has undermined both the hard work that many of us put in to get the state-of-the-art system up and running, and the professional reputation of the Council.

At the moment investigations are on-going, but if you see anything related to this matter, or know of anyone who is abusing and undermining all our hard work, remember that you have a duty of contract to report it immediately to your senior manager. Failure to do this is a sackable offence. We will be issuing regular updates on the situation until the matter is resolved.

Needless to say such actions constitute a sackable offence.

J C Thornton
Project Manager

To: The Administrator
Malbury Centre Health Clinic
43 Green Lanes
Malbury WS2 HH5

3rd August 2003

Dear Sandi pp The Administrator

Thank you for your letter dated 25th July 2003.

Enclosed please find the usual completed Claim For Expenses Form form in the standard sealed envelope.

Could you please send me another Claim For Expenses Form form?

Yours Faithfully

Jim Allbright
J Allbright
32 Pinetree Road
Malbury
WS9 JG8

P.S. Hello Sandi!

Well, you might not get to meet me, but you will get to meet that nasty person James - he got the job. I hope he doesn't turn out too badly. You might get to quite like him over time. (I think I'm becoming schizophrenic here.)

I went through the correspondence - and there's a lot of it for just one poxy window cleaning job - and I couldn't find these rude comments anywhere. Until I looked at the 'James' folder. Someone has definitely been playing silly buggers. But as far as I can see they're between a rock and a hard place; if they insist that no-one can change the system, then Graham can't have done anything. If they say he is responsible, then they're admitting that the system isn't what they promised it would be.

Though, based on my experience in the police force, you're right - they could believe that two plus two makes twenty-seven if they want to. I used to think it was only religious nutters and politicians who could do that - believe something which is obviously false and contradictory - but it seems that all humans do it. Just some are better at it than most of us.

I'm sure Helen is a delightful child, undoubtedly the best in the world. After all, she has such a wonderful and charming mother. I look forward to meeting her.

Do you think I should write to the Auditing department and demand a recount? Maybe I could get the job instead of that James bloke.

How's the internet going?

Jim

P.P.S.

Okay, I admit that thinking that you were a lucky person was my second thought when I first saw you. The first was "I must get to know that beautiful woman".

Oh, and three kisses to little Helen. Would she mind if I sent one or two to her mother?

To: The Senior Administrator
Malbury Centre Health Clinic
43 Green Lanes
Malbury WS2 HH5

3rd August 2003

Dear Senior Administrator Valerie Grateley

Thank you for your letter dated 25th July 2003.

Enclosed please find completed Forms TOC7623, Contract of Signature TOC7622 and Form ACC985, Claim For Expenses in their relevant self-seal pre-paid envelopes.

Could you please send me another Claim For Expenses Form form?

Yours Faithfully

James Allbright

J Allbright
32 Pinetree Road
Malbury WS9 JG8

P.S.

Dear Val

Sounds like you're going to be incredibly busy for a while. Have you thought about a logo for your company? I always find a representation of a bird stays in peoples' minds for some strange reason. Not that I could use it for my company, mind - when people see a bird and a window they get the wrong idea.

Best of luck

James

Malbury Centre Health Clinic

43 Green Lanes, Malbury, WS2 HH5

To: J Allbright
32 Pinetree Road
Malbury WS9 JG8
Reference Code : ALLBRIGHTJIM2003_0000000002

7th August 2003

1. Due to security revalidation the contents of this letter cannot be given.

S Goodwin

pp The Administrator

P.S.

Oh, Jim, you're going to love this one!

In case you're wondering about the funny message, they've decided not to print anything else until they've worked out who's been fiddling with the system. If they can, that is. Meanwhile it would cost too much to have the system changed properly, so they've decided to have it only print the one line, which they can easily see if it's been mucked about with.

Graham reckons they haven't a clue. They've had him on the carpet, almost but not quite accusing him of doing something, but he's just told them that he hasn't done anything, and he couldn't, anyway, because there's no way of changing anything. He thinks it's hilarious. God, he's brave. I wouldn't like to have to face that lot of evil old wotsits. They never smile, you know. Never. Ever.

But from what I've heard from some of the others, they really don't know what to do. The company that supplied the software are insisting that no-one could have hacked into the system. I don't think they know what's going on either, they just know they can't admit it's a pile of rubbish. I'm sure Graham has done something, he can be really childish sometimes. Maybe that's why he and Helen get on so well. The three of us went for a walk yesterday evening down the lake - boy was it hot. Haven't enjoyed an ice-cream like that for ages. Well, two, to be honest. Could have made it three, but Helen would have wanted another as well, and she would have been sick all night. I think I wouldn't have felt so well either.

And then, when I was tucking her into bed she asked me whether I was going to marry Graham, and why wasn't I sleeping with him. Kids! They really ask difficult questions sometimes. I fobbed her off with some story or other. Then when I was turning out the light she said something about how nice it would be to have a real daddy, like the daddy I tell her I had. Almost broke my heart, poor little thing. I sat in the kitchen and looked at the ceiling, trying to imagine Dad was up there somewhere, and asking him to make it better, like he did when I was a kid. There you go, I'm starting to blubber again.

God, I can be a daft cow sometimes. I promise that isn't like me at all. I hardly ever do that sort of thing. Probably just as well I'm not going out with Graham. All my boyfriends seem to end up in trouble if not jail, and he's in enough trouble as it is. And he's too much of a sweetie for that.

Do, do write to the Ethical Oversight Department and complain. They're another bunch of humourless aliens. They'll probably have a full investigation and then decide to give you the job. And I'd much rather meet you than that other bloke. Even if it is you as well. Though he isn't, if you know what I mean.

So when will you be around these parts for an after-work drink? Helen wants to know when she's going to meet my mystery man.

And her mother does not object to her one or two kisses, apart from the small amount offered (just joking).

Sandi

xxx

P.P.S.

Almost forgot the address for the Ethical Oversight Department. Just write ' Ethical Oversight Department', and then the usual council address. Not a lot of people know that.

43 Green Lanes, Malbury, WS2 HH5

To: J Allbright
32 Pinetree Road
Malbury WS9 JG8
Reference Code : ALLBRIGHTJAMES2003_0000000002

7th August 2003

1. Due to security revalidation the contents of this letter cannot be given.

V Grateley

V Grateley
Senior Administrator

P.S.

My Dear James

Apologies for the terseness of the official letter. It's about the start date of the contract, but we're currently running an investigation into abuse of our computer systems, so we have to be careful what we allow through. I know who the culprit is, but unfortunately Council rules are quite strict on the issue of proof. Far too strict, I think. It's a throwback to the bad old days of the unions. I certainly will not have that nonsense in my company.

Many thanks for the idea of the logo. Jane agrees that some form of bird would be ideal - flying high, as an image. A conceptual bird, obviously. Vince thinks it should have echoes of the dove of peace, though I'm not quite sure where that fits in. Apparently, because of the situation in the Middle East, and terrorism, and that sort of thing, people are subconsciously attracted by symbols of peace. That isn't my field, so I will have to accept it - Vince is an professional in that field, after all.

He's introduced me to an expert in feng shui. I have to admit to being sceptical about that sort of thing previously, but it's quite amazing when you speak to an expert rather than reading these critical articles in the press. Being an expert, they charge a hefty fee, but you do get what you pay for, and I am learning a lot about that area.

Yours Sincerely

Valerie Grateley, C-Girl!

xx

P.P.S.

Programme will go out on the 1st September - provisionally, at the moment. Wish me luck.

To: The Ethical Oversight Department
Malbury Council Centre
Park Road
Malbury WS8 HT9

10th August 2003

Dear Ethical Oversight Person

REF : ALLBRIGHTJIM2003_0000000002

I have received a letter from the Council advising me that my tender for contract has not been accepted. However no reason was given. It would obviously be of great beneficial help to me if I understood the reasons behind this, so that in any possible future tender I could meet Malbury Council's exacting and professional standards.

I would be most grateful if you could look into the affair so that I can rest assured that the tendering process was above board, and that Malbury Council's reputation for applying a level playing field approach has been maintained.

Could you please send me Form ACC985 and its relevant sealable envelope?

Yours Faithfully

Jim Allbright

J Allbright
32 Pinetree Road
Malbury WS9 JG8

To: The Administrator
Malbury Centre Health Clinic
43 Green Lanes
Malbury WS2 HH5

10th August 2003

Dear Sandi pp The Administrator

Thank you for your letter dated 7th August 2003.

Unfortunately I did not understand a word of it. Could you let me know the contents without breaking security requirements?

Enclosed please find the usual completed Claim For Expenses Form form in the standard sealed envelope.

Could you please send me another Claim For Expenses Form form?

Yours Faithfully

Jim Allbright
J Allbright
32 Pinetree Road
Malbury WS9 JG8

P.S.

Dear Sandi

Have they completely taken leave of their senses? How can you send out letters which contain only the message that they can't tell you what would have been in the letter? Are they doing this to everyone? The mind boggles. I got a letter from your beloved colleague which was supposed to give the start date of the contract, but of course it didn't. Do you suppose they'll take me to court for breach of contract? If they do they won't be able to tell me. Maybe this is what George Orwell was on about, only weirder.

I've written a letter to the Ethical Oversight department. I don't know if they'll reply, and if they do, will I know what they're saying, or will it be another security message?

It is hard on kids with only one parent. These days you would have thought it not uncommon, but I suppose they know who their father is, even if the parents aren't together. Have you told Helen who her father is and why he isn't there?

Tell her the mystery man can't wait to meet her.

Sounds like Graham doesn't go a whole ball on authority. It also sounds like he should find another job. Surely in his line of work there must be hundreds of other opportunities?

I'm meeting Kayley for a drink round your way on Thursday. What say we all get together? There's a pub called the Goose a block away, supposed to be quite nice. We'll be there from about six till seven.

Looking forward to meeting you.

Jim

P.P.S.

Lovely weather, isn't it? Hottest recorded temperature ever. Everybody else complains - even Kayley - but I reckon it's fantastic, especially if you can just sit in the shade with a good book and a pint.

The Senior Administrator
Malbury Centre Health Clinic
43 Green Lanes
Malbury WS2 HH5

10th August 2003

Dear Senior Administrator Valerie Grateley

Thank you for your letter dated 7th August 2003.

I'm led to believe it should have contained details of the start date of the contract. Unfortunately this was not the case. Could you let me know the correct date?

Enclosed please find the usual completed Claim For Expenses Form form in the standard sealed envelope.

Could you please send me another Claim For Expenses Form form?

Yours Faithfully

James Allbright

J Allbright
32 Pinetree Road
Malbury WS9 JG8

P.S.

Dear Val

Sorry to hear of the problems you're having with your computers. It's probably one of those viruses. I made a decision many years ago to stay with a paper-based system purely for that reason. I can understand the Council requiring a computer system, but I've known companies which have gone under because what started off as a small computer department ended up taking up almost the whole budget, and they forgot what the original purpose of the company was.

I shall have to look into this feng shui question. I'm sure a couple dotted around the office will make it look more relaxed.

I'll keep my eyes on the schedules for the programme.

Best of luck

James

Malbury Centre Health Clinic

43 Green Lanes, Malbury, WS2 HH5

To: J Allbright
32 Pinetree Road
Malbury WS9 JG8
Reference Code : ALLBRIGHTJIM2003_0000000002

15th August 2003

1. For security reasons we cannot print the contents of this letter. You must contact our Customer Care department in Malbury Centre in person with this letter and a form of identification such as passport for this information.

S Goodwin

pp The Administrator

P.S. Hiya Jim!

I don't think they've taken leave of their senses, I don't think they had any to take care of in the first place. Fortunately you're about the only person I have to write to - seeing as we have hardly any patients left - but apparently all hell was let loose at the Council head office. People phoning up to find out what their letters meant, some people thinking that there had been some sort of terrorist attack, all sorts of strange ideas. Now, as you can see, they've made a slight improvement. All you have to do is go to head office with your passport. Which will be a little bit of a problem if you're housebound, or a pensioner without transport, or live the other side of town. Or don't have a passport. And Customer Care aren't too happy, from what I hear. They've only got two people, and they aren't the brightest I've ever met.

I've never met anyone from the Ethical Oversight Department - no-one I've met has ever met anyone from there. Sometimes I wonder if they exist. But we do get the occasional letter from them, so I suppose they must exist. But they never give names on their letters, only 'Senior Ethical Oversight Manager', or 'Assistant Ethical Oversight Manager', so what will happen to your letter I haven't a clue.

I haven't told Helen who her father is, or that he's in jail. When she first asked I just said that he had to go away and wouldn't be coming back. I suppose I'll have to tell her one day.

Helen's really looking forward to meeting you. She can have some funny moods sometimes, though. When I told her what you said she just shrugged and asked when Uncle Graham was coming around. Children do that sometimes, pretend they aren't interested when they really are.

I hope she hasn't become too attached to Graham. He's talking about moving to Brighton to find a job. Apparently even the computer market is having problems at the moment. And having worked for a Council doesn't look too good on your CV, so he tells me. But he reckons he could find something in Brighton, and he says he likes the place. For some reason he asked whether it's the sort of place I'd like to live. I've lived all my life here, never thought of moving anywhere else. Thinking about it, I suppose I might like it, with the sea so close by. I like the sea, and I know Helen does. Ah, well, maybe some other time. Would you like to live near the sea?

Sorry I missed you on Thursday. Typical, I had arranged a babysitter and everything, and Helen comes down with something and just won't stop crying because Mummy's going to leave her when she's so ill, so in the end I had to promise I'd stay and look after her. I told Graham, and he came around to read her stories, so she managed to forget how sick she was, which was something of a godsend.

Graham has to attend a disciplinary meeting next week. They can't prove he had something to do with the funny messages on the letters, so they've decided that he has an attitude problem. I think it has something to do with him telling them that their system was rubbish. He's only saying what everybody else thinks.

Tell you what, instead of arranging a time to meet up, why don't you give me a call at work when you're going to be around this way - ask one of the security guards to tell me you're outside, they won't let you in without a pass.

At least then fate won't have a chance to mess things up.

Sandi

xxx

P.P.S. No, it was far too hot. I love sunny days, but last week was just way too hot.

P.P.S. Brilliant news. That silly old cow is leaving! We're planning on a celebration. Without her, of course.

Malbury Centre Health Clinic Senior Administrators' Department

43 Green Lanes, Malbury, WS2 HH5

To: J Allbright

32 Pinetree Road

Malbury WS9 JG8

Reference Code : ALLBRIGHTJAMES2003_0000000002

15th August 2003

1. For security reasons we cannot print the contents of this letter. Please contact our Customer Care department in Malbury Centre in person with a form of identification such as passport for this information.

V Grateley

Senior Administrator

P.S.

Dear James

You were absolutely right about the virus. The software company providing the system were a bit sceptical at first, but we're confident that it is this MSBlaster virus that the media have highlighted recently. One of our senior managers has a nephew who is an expert in these things, and he came in to clean the system up. We have decided to contract his company to look after the security of our network. The other company are extremely good at what they do, but I'm afraid things such as viruses are not their area of expertise.

Jane and I have formally handed in our notice. Everyone is quite sad that we're leaving, and obviously they're concerned about recruiting the right calibre of individuals to replace us. There are so few really good project co-ordinators around.

Yours Sincerely

Valerie Grateley, C-Girl!

xx

Internal E-Mail

Private And Confidential

From : J C Thornton

To : All Council Staff

cc : Peter V Hamilton

Sent : 09:15:23 20th August 2003

After much hard work and the aid of professional technical experts we have tracked down the cause of the recent problems within the system. As you will all know from news reports a serious computer virus has been causing problems for many companies. It appears that someone has not followed Council procedures and has allowed this virus to enter our systems. Fortunately, after a series of out-of-hours sessions we have been able to eradicate the problem.

However this does not mean that the danger has passed. We must be eternally vigilant, as these attacks will not stop. To prevent further infections occurring we have taken on the expert help of CompSols, a company specialising in security issues. We are also in discussion with them regarding the supply of Council computers, printers and associated computer requirements, and hope to achieve a marked reduction in costs, as well as improvement in quality.

There are other preventative measures we can take. A high-level decision has been made to further restrict access to all e-mails, both internal and external, to those for whom it is essential. From today on the only staff permitted to use e-mail facilities will be those of grade C1 and above, i.e. senior managers and senior administrative staff.

I would like to take this opportunity to thank everyone, on behalf of myself and Valerie Grateley, for the many good wishes on the start of our own company, C-Girls. You may be aware that the BBC will be featuring a documentary on the development of the company, expected to be shown around the 1st of September.

Valerie and I have thoroughly enjoyed our time here with the Council, and leave in place a system that we can all be truly proud of. I feel I can say with confidence that you will all maintain the high standards people have come to expect of Malbury Council.

J C Thornton

Project Manager

MALBURY COUNCIL ETHICAL OVERSIGHT DEPARTMENT

Internal E-Mail

Private And Confidential

From : Senior Manager, Ethical Oversight Department

To : J C Thornton

Sent : 14:00:00 20th August 2003

An audit of the failed contract tender of ALLBRIGHTJIM 2003_0000000002 is in process.

We note that staff member Grateley, Valerie has left details on file of the head of the company's political affiliations. Council rules specifically forbid any member of staff acting with political bias. Current systems are designed to prevent this happening.

As Grateley, Valerie reports directly to yourself we would like an explanation of this breach of Council rules.

Senior Ethical Monitor

Malbury Council Project Services

Internal E-Mail

Private And Confidential

From : J C Thornton

To : Graham Pinder

cc : Peter V Hamilton

Sent : 10:45:01 21st August 2003

As per our discussion this is a formal, written warning concerning your current conduct and behaviour which we, in committee, have judged to be disruptive and unacceptable.

The committee has fairly and evenly listened to your side, and finds your evidence to be unreliable.

A further warning will result in automatic and instant dismissal.

J C Thornton
Project Manager

GWAJAMWATU

General Workers Apprentices Journeymen Artisans Mens and Womens
Affiliated Trade Union

External E-Mail

Private And Confidential

From : Joseph Parker, General Secretary, Malbury Branch,
GWAJAMWATU

To : Sir Henry Walters

Sent : 15:22:58 21st August 2003

Dear Sir Henry

Following our discussion at lunch, I am writing to you formally to state that
we consider the recent treatment of our member Graham Pinder
unacceptable and effectively constructive dismissal, and will be seeking an
industrial tribunal's ruling in the affair.

Yours Faithfully

Joe Parker
General Secretary, Malbury Branch, GWAJAMWAT

Delete the rest of this as per usual just to be on the safe side.

I've been phoning around some of our members who work for the council,
and they're not a happy lot. They sound like they need only a small excuse
to go out on strike. Whether they'd do it for some stroppy computer nerd I
don't know, but it looks quite possible. Personally I blame it on the
weather. People aren't used to this heat, they get irritable and uppity. I
reckon we'll be seeing the French farmers out blocking the streets soon like

they usually do, protesting the price of garlic or whatever. As I said at lunch, probably best to call it a misunderstanding, sling the kid a few quid, and get rid of him. I don't know what he's doing in our union in the first place, these computer geeks are hardly the starving workers or members of the people's proletariat, what with the salaries they earn. Trouble is he's been talking to one of our lawyers, Shaftcliff, and you know what happened the last time he got involved. No understanding of politics. Right pain in the neck.

Oh, while I remember, I won't be able to make our golf round tomorrow afternoon, I've got to meet the Shafter tomorrow about this thing, tried to get out of it, or the time changed, but he won't have it - I swear he checked my diary. Said something about our members being more important than a game of golf. Sarky bastard. I'll send my secretary to make up the four, you know, the one with the nice bum who can't play golf for toffee.

Regards
Joe

To: The Administrator

Malbury Centre Health Clinic

43 Green Lanes

Malbury WS2 HH5

24th August 2003

Dear Sandi pp The Administrator

Thank you for your letter dated 15th August 2003.

I contacted your Customer Care department regarding your last letter, but unfortunately they were unable to supply me with any information. Could you possibly enlighten me?

Enclosed please find the usual completed Claim For Expenses Form form in the standard sealed envelope.

Could you please send me another Claim For Expenses Form form?

Yours Faithfully

Jim Allbright

J Allbright

32 Pinetree Road

Malbury WS9 JG8

P.S.

Dear Sandi

I'm beginning to wonder whether I'm living in the real world or whether this is just some terrible nightmare - and will I wake up eventually? Went around to your Customer Care department early on the morning of the 20th. There's a regular once-a-week job at Vaidoo's mini-supermarket that I have to do at six in the morning. He - Vaidoo - thinks it's bad for business if his clients see his windows being washed, don't know why, but he has some funny ideas of how the English expect people to behave. I think he longs to be what he thinks of as an English Gentleman. Doesn't bother me, I like being up early in this weather, and he coughs up a decent amount without arguing. Probably knows he couldn't get anyone else to do the job that early if at all.

Anyway, so I finished Vaidoo's place, and decided to nip off to the Customer Care department and see if they were open. They weren't - it was about still only about eight o'clock - but there was already a queue of five people waiting, and they weren't happy. So I got myself a take-away tea and joined the queue to find out what was going on, and by then there were about fifteen people. Turns out that everyone who does work for or has anything to do with the council has been getting these letters about turning up at Customer Care to discover the mystery message. There was a baker who was there early because he normally starts baking at four in the morning; he didn't know whether the council catering department needed the usual, or was there a special function on, or what. They wouldn't tell him over the phone - for 'security reasons', and these were people he's known for years - and he didn't know how much flour and suchlike to order. Said that these days things are so tight you can't afford to have perishable goods hanging around going off.

The others had pretty much similar problems - how can you plan ahead if you don't know what's going on? There was an Irish builder there who was cussing fit to burst - someone has crashed into a council house - not many of those left. He didn't know whether he only had to rebuild a front wall with two of his 'boys', or replace the entire front of a house which would take eight, including people like electricians and plumbers. And then you had parents who had just moved into the area wanting to know which school their kids would be going to. And confused pensioners. And anyone you could possibly imagine who might have had to speak to the council. By the time the office opened at nine the queue went right round the block, including ill people waiting for news of their doctor's appointments.

When I got in I found they worked one of those systems where you take a ticket and wait for your number to be called, so I acted pro-actively as they call it. I took four tickets. When my first number came up I went up and asked about the Jim account. Boy, the two people behind the counter - like a bank, with bullet-proof glass - did not look happy. And, like you said, I don't think they'd give Einstein sleepless nights. Mickey Mouse could beat them in the cranial department. Anyway, the one I'm talking to has a dig into a pile of letters on a desk behind him; there were several desks, and several piles, but he only checked the one. They weren't alphabetical or anything, I could tell from the names and reference numbers I spotted, all over the place.

He comes back and tells me they haven't received anything yet, which looks like the approach they've decided to take. Have a quick look, if the punter - sorry, customer - is really, really lucky their letter will be somewhere obvious, like floating in the air in front of their face with a brick attached. Otherwise say, 'Sorry, not here, next please' and call out the next number. And because I'd taken a set of numbers one of them was the next number, so I got to ask about the James account too - no way was I going to join the back of the queue just for that - it would have taken the whole day. The bloke was a bit confused, but didn't stop to think, just went and rooted around in the same pile, and, miracle of miracles, found the letter. All it says is that I start washing your surgery window 1st September and thereafter once a week on a weekly basis, contract renewable every six months. All that palava over one window. It's cost them a fortune so far and the glass has yet to smell so much as a dribble of cleaning liquid.

Haven't heard from the Ethical department. To be honest, I don't expect to. When I've had dealings with the council previously it seemed like all my letters disappeared into a black hole, and that's what will happen with them, if they exist. Though this new system of yours does seem to have made sure that letters get answered. The result is the same - nothing happens - but at least the letters get answered.

Brighton's a pretty good place if you've got the money. I lived there for six months once, had a great time. Do you think Graham is trying to tell you something by asking you whether you like the area?

How's the internet doing? Your new computer hasn't caught anything has it?

I think you'll have to tell Helen the truth sooner or later. Maybe when she's a bit older though. You never know what affect that sort of thing has on kids.

I wouldn't worry about Graham's disciplinary. We had loads of them when I was on the force. Hardly anything came of them. Most of the time it was just some senior officer who suspected that one - or more - of us had been bending the rules a little. So long as they couldn't prove anything we just said yes sir, no sir, three bags full sir and laughed it off.

So, we shall finally meet on the 1st September. Who would have believed such a simple thing could take so long?

Looking forward to it.

Love

Jim

To: The Senior Administrator
Malbury Centre Health Clinic
43 Green Lanes
Malbury WS2 HH5

24th August 2003

Dear Senior Administrator Valerie Grateley

Thank you for your letter dated 15th August 2003.

Enclosed please find the usual completed Claim For Expenses Form form in the standard sealed envelope.

Could you please send me another Claim For Expenses Form form?

Yours Faithfully

James Allbright

J Allbright
32 Pinetree Road
Malbury WS9 JG8

P.S.

Dear Val

Good to hear you sorted the virus problem. I presume you will have state-of-the-art computer systems in your new company? They cost a bit, but with computers it's all or nothing.

I can understand the council's concern over the losing of two such qualified staff. But surely the system has been bedded down now, so to speak. Would they require highly qualified computer people to run it?

You know, they should lock up these people who create computer viruses, and throw away the key.

Best of luck

James

Malbury Centre Health Clinic

43 Green Lanes, Malbury, WS2 HH5

To: J Allbright
32 Pinetree Road
Malbury WS9 JG8
Reference Code : ALLBRIGHTJIM2003_0000000002

27th August 2003

To : J Allbright

1. Thank you for your letter concerning Glazing Maintenance Project, Reference KL/000001/AE/9/4.3.

2. As per your request I enclose Form ACC985, Claim For Expenses. You must return the form in the pre-paid envelope.

S Goodwin

pp The Administrator

P.S.

Jim!

(Was just thinking the other day what a sweet name Jimmy would be for a baby boy. I'll bet you were a sweet little baby!)

Well, one good thing about the security scare is that they've cut out all the extra print-outs and whatnots, just left the basic stuff in. Apparently it would have cost too much too have them put back in, and they can't afford it at the moment. And with the old cow leaving that hopefully will never happen. We've had an e-mail telling us that it was caused by a virus - whatever 'it' was, and I don't think they know. Graham says it's a load of rubbish; the virus they're blaming - MSBlaster I think it's called, strange name - only appeared a few days ago. And it doesn't corrupt systems, just knocks networks out by trying to dial Microsoft the whole time. And none of the machines he checked had it. He reckons the new company - they've hired 'specialists' to look after computer security - don't know what they're talking about.

Not that he's doing too well - Graham, I mean. They sent him an e-mail as a formal warning about his behaviour, he took it to the union, and now they're threatening the council with an industrial tribunal and god knows what else. I can't see him staying on at the council, and he won't find it easy getting another job if he's been involved in an industrial tribunal.

He doesn't seem too worried though. Came around to my place to check that my computer didn't have the new virus - or one of the new viruses, apparently there are two or three new bad ones flying around. Gave me a lecture on keeping my anti-virus software up to date, never thought of him as the stern type. Quite sexy in a funny way. Helen thinks the world of him, even when he's been stern. Asks me every day whether I've 'done my anti-virus computer stuff like uncle Graham said'. Threatened to phone Graham if I didn't. I hope she grows out of it, it's amusing at first but I think it will drive me crazy after a week.

Still, Graham will no doubt be off to Brighton once this business with the council is sorted, so I suppose that's the last I'll see of him. Typical. Men!

Not you, of course.

Graham is the only real friend I have, apart from you - and I haven't even met you - and now he'll soon be gone.

I'm a silly cow. That's makes it sound as if I'm feeling sorry for myself. I'll shut up about that. Dad always used to say that the worst thing you can do is feel sorry for yourself. And he was right. So I won't.

How's Kayley keeping? Are you still going out?

Customer Care should have the backlog cleared by about sometime next century. A friend of mine in council head office says everyone is blaming everyone else, Customer Care is being accused of 'not being able to do the simplest job', they're saying they didn't have the resources and weren't involved in the planning so didn't know what they were supposed to do, etc, etc, etc. They have a point. They may be thick as two bricks, but they do have a point. Meanwhile the two most involved in the mess are leaving at the end of the month, so we can all settle down afterwards, and hopefully start to act normally.

I'd hoped to take Helen away for the long weekend, but, guess what, most of the trains were cancelled due to engineering work. Which they only told us about two days before. Had a long row with one of their people, who told me that 'the information had been in the public domain for months'. I don't care where it's been for months, nobody told us until two days before. Helen suggested we ask Graham to drive us somewhere - he's got quite a nice car, one of those people-carriers or whatever they're called, lovely dark-blue colour, don't ask me what model or make. Course I couldn't do that, ask him to take us out just like that, it wouldn't be fair on him. So Helen - would you believe it - asked him when he was around instead, she can really be a forward little thing when she wants to. He just laughed and said yes, if we left a day early and came back a day late. Since that was Friday it was already too late. He explained to her how everybody tried to rush away for a long weekend, spent ages in traffic jams, and ended up being very unhappy and upset with everyone else, so it was better to stay at home and take things easy. Because it was Graham who said it of course she accepted it without a word of complaint. Decided we'd spend the weekend going to the park and that sort of thing, Helen likes that.

One day Graham will have kids of his own and they won't believe a word he says and it will serve him right.

Things seem a little gloomy at the moment. Maybe it's because we haven't had this sunny weather they've been promising. Maybe it's because it's August and winter's on its way.

Oh, well, at least one ray of light. We shall finally get to meet each other on September 1st. I shall make a special note in my diary. I'm really looking forward to it.

Love

Sandi

xxx

P.P.S.

The Old Moo is having farewell drinks in the Metier on Friday, that snotty wine bar off Havelock Street. We're having our own celebration in the George and Dragon. We might paint out the dragon, sort of symbolically.

Malbury Centre Health Clinic Senior Administrators' Department

43 Green Lanes, Malbury, WS2 HH5

To: J Allbright

32 Pinetree Road

Malbury WS9 JG8

Reference Code : ALLBRIGHTJAMES2003_0000000002

27th August 2003

1. Thank you for your letter concerning Glazing Maintenance Project, Reference KL/000001/AE/9/4.3.

2. As per your request I enclose Form ACC985, Claim For Expenses. You must return the form in the pre-paid envelope.

Yours Sincerely

V Grateley

Senior Administrator

P.S.

My Dear James

This is probably the last chance I will have to write to you, as Friday is the last day I work for the Council. We'll be having farewell drinks in the French cafe; off Havelock Street, the Metier, I'm sure you know it, it's one of the few decent wine bars here. Please come if you can make it - it seems strange that we've been writing to each other for so long, and we haven't ever actually met.

You're quite right about computers and the Council systems. We have already ordered the best money can buy for our new company, including overhead projectors, massive LCD screens, you name it. It's cost a fortune, but you have to spend a lot to make the right impression. And as far as the Council systems go, yes, now that we have built them up properly, they only really need maintaining, so I suppose the Council will no longer require a highly-trained and professional project management team.

There's a strange mood in the air; Jane and I are terribly excited, everyone is wishing us well, but at the same time there is a certain feeling of regret, as if a story is coming to an end. Maybe it's just Autumn. After the August Bank Holiday everything seems to race downhill towards winter and Christmas. Silly, really, after all, we're really entering a whole new story, full of promise and success.

Best of luck for the future, take care.

Yours Sincerely

Valerie Grateley, C-Girl!

xx

Malbury Town Council

External E-Mail

Private And Confidential

From : Sir Henry Walters

To : Joseph Parker, General Secretary, Malbury Branch, GWAJAMWATU

Sent : 11:45:20 28th August 2003

Dear Mr Parker

Many thanks for your communication of 21st August.

Needless to say we take these issues extremely seriously; as you know, we strongly believe that people are our most important resource. It is unfortunate that this matter was not brought to my attention earlier, as an industrial tribunal would not be in anyone's interest, least that of the employee concerned. I will, therefore, be conducting an internal investigation into the matter. I am sure we will be able to resolve the issue amicably and internally.

I look forward to discussing this with you further at our weekly meeting tomorrow afternoon. Many thanks for sending your secretary in your place last week. Her form is certainly improving.

Regards
Henry
Sir Henry Walters
Chairman, Malbury Town Council

To: The Administrator
Malbury Centre Health Clinic
43 Green Lanes
Malbury WS2 HH5

31st August 2003

Dear Sandi pp The Administrator

Thank you for your letter dated 27th August 2003.

Enclosed please find the usual completed Claim For Expenses Form form in the standard sealed envelope.

Could you please send me another Claim For Expenses Form form?

Yours Faithfully

Jim Allbright
J Allbright
32 Pinetree Road
Malbury WS9 JG8

P.S.

Dear Sandi

Makes me glad I don't have a computer. Can you imagine buying a car that had to be fixed up or patched up every few days because someone on the other side of the world has invented a new virus? Come to think of it, these days cars all have computer chips in them anyway, don't they? God, that's a horrible thought. You're doing 100 mile an hour down the motorway and your car suddenly locks up because of a virus some spotty kid in California has written for kicks. I'll make a note only to buy fully manual in future.

To be honest my van is so old and manual sometimes I have to get out and push the bloody thing.

Sounds like Graham is in way over his head. I would have thought he would just accept a reprimand, laugh it off. I used to get them all the time. Well, every few months, anyway. Though I suppose a written warning is a lot more serious than a verbal ticking off. Why did the council go that far? Sounds like someone lost their sense of humour.

Have to agree with him about going away for long weekends though. I've never gone away for a long weekend since a bad experience in Blackpool. Traffic was murderous - parked up for miles. Hot as anything. The wife - ex-wife, now - was even more pissed off than usual. When we finally made it into the town, four hours late, frazzled, nerves on razorblades, we found that our chosen B&B was not the height of luxury we thought we were paying for - and it wasn't cheap - but a total dump. Smelled of stale cooking and beer (don't know where the beer smell came from, the woman running it had a husband who drank whisky from waking up until falling over, but I never saw any beer). Toilets were filthy, showers made you feel more dirty after the shower than before - you name it, all the horrors possible. We ended up going home before the end of the weekend, everywhere else was full, and we decided we'd rather be miserable at home.

The wife left me two weeks later, so maybe it was worth it.

Kayley is, you could say, as fit as a fiddle. She was working in the pub Friday evening, so I nipped in for a pint. She wasn't in a good mood though, and she'd had a couple of glasses of wine before starting which seemed to make things worse - what the ex used to call 'having the red flag flying', only the with the ex you'd think she was a permanent paid up member of the Communist party - so I sat at a table in the corner and read a paper while waiting for her shift to finish. At a table nearby there were a couple of sad young blokes, cheap and nasty deodorant, cheap and flashy suits, needed a shower and a haircut and a new attitude, one full of himself, the other believing his mate's drivel, you know the sort. They work in a tatty little estate agency a couple of blocks away, only drop in on Fridays to have a couple of pints and tell each other how important they are - well the first one does that to the other. Among his more memorable quotes are "if anyone gets in my way I trample all over them", and "if I see something I want I take it, including women". Not exactly everybody's cup of tea, and definitely not Kayley's. So it was probably a mistake on big-mouth's part to pat her on the backside as she came around removing empty glasses and clearing ashtrays. Before you could say "excuse me" he was on his face, on the ground, pausing only briefly as his face hit the table and went through it - Kayley's not only a big girl, she's also done some martial arts stuff. I did think putting the boot in was a little unnecessary, especially seeing as where she put it into. I don't think he'll be walking properly for a few days.

I was sitting there quietly minding my own business - albeit with a rather large grin on my face - and she looks at me and says "And I don't want to hear a word from you". Well, as if I would. I wasn't even thinking of complaining about certain drunken people resorting to unnecessary violence

Pete got the police in to remove the lad (they refused to get him an ambulance), though not before getting rid of the last of the worm-eaten stools in the back storage room. That man has a cheek you have to admire.

See you tomorrow. (Probably before you get this letter.)

Love

Jim

To: The Senior Administrator
Malbury Centre Health Clinic
43 Green Lanes
Malbury WS2 HH5

31st August 2003

Dear Senior Administrator Valerie Grateley (or whoever has taken over)

Thank you for your letter dated 27th August 2003.

Enclosed please find the usual completed Claim For Expenses Form form in the standard sealed envelope.

Could you please send me another Claim For Expenses Form form?

Yours Faithfully

James Allbright

J Allbright
32 Pinetree Road
Malbury WS9 JG8

Malbury Council Accounts Department

Malbury Council Centre, Park Road, Malbury, WS8 HT9

To: J Allbright

32 Pinetree Road

Malbury WS9 JG8

Reference Code : ALLBRIGHTJIM2003_0000000002

1st September 2003

1. Notification of payment

Details : General expenses payment, breakdown attached

2. Payee : Jim Allbright

3. Account details : As specified in breakdown

4. Date of payment : 31/08/2003

5. Amount : £489.30 (Four hundred and eighty-nine punds and thirty pence)

6. Accruals : £None (None)

7. Accrual Basis : Monthly interest

8. Method of Payment : Electronic Transfer

9. Contest : If you wish to contest this payment you must contact Malbury Services Auditing Department. This Department is unable to enter into any correspondence with you over this matter.

10. Declaration : This payment has been automatically generated by our computer services. The amounts may not be muddified.

Malbury Council Accounts Department

Malbury Council Centre, Park Road, Malbury, WS8 HT9

To: J Allbright

32 Pinetree Road

Malbury WS9 JG8

Reference Code : ALLBRIGHTJAMES2003_0000000002

1st September 2003

1. Notification of payment

Details : General expenses payment, breakdown attached

2. Payee : James Allbright

3. Account details : As specified in breakdown

4. Date of payment : 31/08/2003

5. Amount : £388.45 (Three hundred and eighty-eight punds and forty-five pence)

6. Accruals : £None (None)

7. Accrual Basis : Monthly interest

8. Method of Payment : Electronic Transfer

9. Contest : If you wish to contest this payment you must contact Malbury Services Auditing Department. This Department is unable to enter into any correspondence with you over this matter.

10. Declaration : This payment has been automatically generated by our computer services. The amounts may not be muddified.

To: The Senior Administrator

Malbury Centre Health Clinic

43 Green Lanes

Malbury WS2 HH5

1st September 2003

Dear Whoever Has Taken Over From Senior Administrator Valerie Grateley

This morning I went to your clinic to wash the windows as per contract, Reference ALLBRIGHTJAMES2003_0000000002. However the two security guards outside refused to let me anywhere near the place without a Malbury Council security pass.

As I have never been sent such a thing I was unable to produce it, and not even the production of the signed contract would convince them that I was not a dangerous terrorist armed with a lethal bucket and squeegee, capable of creating havoc and a national state of emergency with said weapons. Not to put a fine point on it, they were extremely belligerent, and even downright offensive.

I'd rather not say where the one guard suggested I put my squeegee. We almost had a full and frank exchange of opinions on the point. Could you please send me the necessary information to obtain such a security pass so that I can wash the window legally?

Could you please send me a Claim For Expenses Form form?

Yours Faithfully

James Allbright

J Allbright

32 Pinetree Road

Malbury WS9 JG8

The Herald

2nd September 2003

Last Night's Television

Review by Roger Carlisle

As everyone who reads this column will know, I'm not a fan of so-called 'reality television'. In fact I thoroughly abhor the stuff, partly because it's much more 'television' than reality, and partly because it's undignified watching people flaunt their inadequacies in public. But it has to be said that last night's BBC programme was the exception. It isn't often that I am so fascinated by a programme that I don't touch my drink until the end, but watching *The Way To The Top?* was like watching a particularly gruesome and self-inflicted accident in very slow motion. Just when you think it couldn't get worse it did. Just when you thought the participants couldn't say anything more banal or plainly moronic, they did.

For those of you who missed a televisual feast of absurdity, the programme followed two 'professional' women in their plans to set up their own company. You certainly couldn't accuse the producer of setting them up; they were so unbelievably naive and confident in their own abilities and future no producer would need to lead them anywhere, just switch on the camera and sound and leave it running. Which is what they appear to have done, since there was hardly any camera movement, and the central figures constantly moved in and out of shot, but not, unfortunately for them, out of hearing. Normally I would find that 'technique' extremely irritating, but in this case it worked perfectly. It was as wonky as the participants.

The two concerned had decided to go into business as a computer systems consultancy, so you would expect them to discuss, well, such things as systems and computers. Instead they spent most of their time debating the ideal company colours, furnishing, office space, whether they should have a coffee percolator for waiting clients, should it be able to make cappuccino, and above all, what name this wonderful new company should have. It was like watching two eight-year olds playing at being grown up; you almost felt sorry for them. I would feel sorry for their clients, but, and this is the rub - they didn't have any. None existing, none prospective, and, after last night's performance, I can confidently state that the likelihood of any appearing on their doorstep is exactly nil.

They did decide on a company name eventually: C-Girls. Which, unfortunately, when they pronounced it, came out as "seagulls". And anyone who hires them is likely to get the same treatment seagulls give to the unwary beach walker. To cap it all they chose some representation of what looks like a dead dove as the company logo. All this being on the advice of some American advertising guru who no-one I know has ever heard of. You don't have to be a rocket scientist to work out that a highly successful American advertising guru is hardly likely to decide to settle in an obscure English town to make a living. Unfortunately the two deluded women weren't rocket scientists - that might have been an acceptable excuse.

They did eventually mention computers. Sadly it was when they took the cameraman into their 'computer command room' - which looked suspiciously like it had originally been a loo - and then failed utterly to identify their computer file server, the one which everything else runs off. They were searching for something that looked like a standard PC; instead the file server turned out to be an anonymous thin box with the occasional light flashing, something one of the decorators identified for them. We were assured that all the equipment was "leading edge technology". Pity the people were more bleeding edge.

My jaw finally hit the ground when they got around to discussing staff uniforms. Apparently this was part of their 'forward looking' approach. Other people might call it day-dreaming. Unsurprising, in hindsight, they took a 'policy decision' - as part of their company 'ethos' - that all staff would be required to wear a staff uniform (presumably the same hideous purple colour as their chosen company colour) except for themselves, as they were 'client facing'. You could look at this in a number of ways; if the other, putative, staff would not have to meet clients, why the need for a uniform? And presumably they would be employing real computer people at some stage, if only to tell them where their file server was; people who work with computers do not wear uniforms. Their ideal outfit is jeans and t-shirt, preferably but not necessarily clean, certainly never ironed. Even Billy Gates is known for his informal clothing, and these two haven't a snow flake's chance of emulating him. You would have to be a pretty desperate and poor would-be computer nerd to agree to wear a uniform, indeed even to apply for a job with those two. Never has the phrase 'you do need to be mad to work here' had such resonance.

On the other hand, maybe there is a mathematical simplicity to their decision. All staff apart from them have to wear staff uniforms. They will never be able to hire staff, even should some poor deluded company hire them, so they will never have to spend anything on staff uniforms. But they have the company rule. They can explain that their non-existent staff are wearing non-existent purple uniforms to their non-existent clients.

What does exist however is debt, and I would imagine their bank manager was in a state of numbed shock if he watched the programme. They didn't actually give the figures for what they had ordered - such as special purple wallpaper and purple curtains, special purple sound system for 'reception' - but they kept using phrases such as 'state of the art', which never translates as 'cheap' - more like a combination of 'very expensive' and 'very tacky'.

The programme definitely had a touch of Disney about it, unfortunately not so much Walt as Mickey Mouse. Still, there's a silver lining to every cloud, I suppose. My partner, who lectures in business administration, wants a copy of the programme to show to her students as an example of all the things not to do. I think the BBC will make quite a tidy profit on that programme.

GWAJAMWATU

General Workers Apprentices Journeymen Artisans Mens and Womens
Affiliated Trade Union

External E-Mail

Private And Confidential

From : Joseph Parker, General Secretary, Malbury Branch,
GWAJAMWATU

To : Sir Henry Walters

Sent : 11:02:47 3rd September 2003

Dear Sir Henry

Just a quick note to confirm that the conclusions reached at our intensive
discussions in last week's meeting have largely been confirmed, but a small
adjustment in financial remuneration might be required. If you would be
willing to revise the figures upwards by about 10% I feel confident we can
reach agreement on this issue. If you could let me know in the next few
days I might have good news for our weekly meeting on Friday.

Yours Faithfully
Joe Parker
General Secretary, Malbury Branch, GWAJAMWATU

Delete the rest of this as per usual just to be on the safe side.

As we thought the little sod wants more money. Not that it's just him
though, the Shafter is really behind it. He got one of our accountants to go
through the offer and decided that it didn't match up in accounting terms.
Well of course it didn't, we weren't about to let some computer geek grab
our hard earned cash. I would have had a word with the accountant to give
him a bit of political advice, but it was too late by then, and anyway, what I

know about accountancy you could write on the back of a very small postage stamp.

We might as well sort it out this way, the Shafter is muttering words like 'damages' and 'compensation for stress', and we all know what happens when lawyers start using that sort of language. Bung the brat what he wants, give him a lovely reference as agreed, and the Council will have to foot the bill. It might mean the increase in council tax will have to go up a bit more than intended, or maybe you could close another library, no-one will notice. If the lawyers get involved it will cost a hell of a lot more, and we don't know what the result will be anyway.

I'll send my secretary around with the written proposal. Try to return her before too long, she still has my expenses to do for last month, the lazy cow.

See you on the course Friday.

Regards
Joe

Malbury Centre Health Clinic

43 Green Lanes, Malbury, WS2 HH5

To: J Allbright

32 Pinetree Road

Malbury WS9 JG8

Reference Code : ALLBRIGHTJAMES2003_0000000002

4th September 2003

To : J Allbright

1. Thank you for your letter concerning Glazing Maintenance Project, Reference KL/000001/AE/9/4.3.

2. You will have received Form SC8712 and details of how to apply for security clearance as part of your contract agreement. For security reasons this cannot be reprinted. If you have lost the form you will need to reapply for the contract.

Yours Sincerely

S Goodwin

pp The Administrator

P.S.

To: Mr James Allbright

I'm not talking to you, you're the nasty one wot belongs to the National Front.

And now I've got to clear up the old moo's leftover work.

Sandi

P.P.S.

Have enclosed the Expenses form, even if you don't deserve it.

Malbury Centre Health Clinic

43 Green Lanes, Malbury, WS2 HH5

To: J Allbright
32 Pinetree Road
Malbury WS9 JG8
Reference Code : ALLBRIGHTJIM2003_0000000002

4th September 2003

To : J Allbright

1. Thank you for your letter concerning Glazing Maintenance Project, Reference KL/000001/AE/9/4.3.

2. As per your request I enclose Form ACC985, Claim For Expenses. You must return the form in the pre-paid envelope.

Yours Sincerely

S Goodwin
pp The Administrator

P.S.

Jim! My dear, dear Jim! My remaining link to sanity!

I don't believe it! Things finally get sorted out, we're due to meet, and then it turns out that that stupid cow forgot to send you the security application. How she managed that I don't know, it's part of the standard printout, horrible bright orange colour just to make sure people don't miss it. Trouble is that it can't be reprinted - security again, security today, security tomorrow, security for evermore, it's enough to drive you crazy.

I've been through the old cow's files - typical, she left them all in her office for someone else to sort out - and found the ALLBRIGHTJAMES2003_0000000002 one, but the security application wasn't in it. You can't miss them, like I say, they're bright orange. I'd have a word with Dr Singh, but he's on holiday. In fact I'm the only one in this week, apart from the security guards, and they're outside. I would speak to someone at main office, but the council don't publish a telephone list, for security reasons, naturally, and the receptionist who answers the council hot-line won't put me through to anyone because the hot-line is for council residents, not employees, and they've taken our e-mail away. It's weird. You're living in the middle of hundreds of thousands of people and you can't talk to any of them. I read a book about that once, only got half way through because it sounded too weird and silly. Wished I'd finished it now.

Still, don't worry, I'll go round to the main office today and see what I can sort out. My security card won't let me in, but I know a couple of people who work there, I'll try grab them when they come out for lunch.

I think I must have been lucky as far as B&Bs go. You hear all these horror stories, but I've never had a bad experience. Maybe it's one of these cosmic type things, you know, where certain people always have the same luck with certain things. Like when I go to the laundromat I always seem to get the machine which doesn't work, only you only find out after it's taken your money.

The computer's working like a dream, the one Graham gave me. Much faster than the ones at work. And it just sort of feels better, if you know what I mean, like it's better quality. It sounds silly, cause I wouldn't have a clue what quality would be in a computer, but I think this one's got it. I've been really good about following Graham's instructions about what not to do - you know, he told me not to go searching for porn sites and that sort of thing. As if I would, cheeky bugger. But I have to admit I probably would have if he hadn't told me not to. Well, you know, just to see what the fuss is all about. But I don't want my brand new little computer (I call him Alf) catching a virus from places like that. And I don't want anything nasty anywhere near my little Helen.

Graham is happy enough. I don't know why, I don't know why he still goes to work, whatever the tribunal rules he's likely to be out of a job. I'd be worried stiff, but he's quite happy to come over and read Helen bed-time stories. Maybe that's it. If I lose my job it's not just me who suffers, it's my beautiful Helen as well. Graham doesn't have any children to worry about. I reckon if I didn't have Helen I wouldn't give a toss either. Still, I'd rather have Helen and worry, you know?

Sigh. Maybe that's what Dad meant about me being lucky. He never had much, we were pretty poor even by the standards of the Estate, but he always said he was the richest man alive because he had such a wonderful wife and such beautiful daughters.

Admittedly that was when he was well pissed, but, having Helen with me, I can see what he meant.

Kayley sounds like a handful. Some of these Australians are strange. Though, thinking about it, the Yanks are pretty odd, the French have a problem, the Germans are weird, and quite a few of our lot are stark raving bonkers. I suppose all countries have their fair share of weirdoes.

I'll have to rush if I'm going to catch them coming out for lunch at the main office.

Love

Sandi

xxx

P.P.S. have just got back from the main office, all sorted, orange security application enclosed, which means what I wrote above will be a little confusing, so let me explain.

I was waiting outside the main office doors hoping a girl I know - not too well, but anywhere's a start - would come out. Instead Graham walks out, and I think, of course, silly cow, he works at main office and I've got his mobile number, why didn't I think of asking him? The office phone won't let us call a mobile, but I could have used the call-box up the street, providing it wasn't kicked in yet again.

I suppose, it's like when you get thinking one way you can't help but think that way, if you see what I mean. I was thinking I needed to speak to someone in admin about a security pass, so I didn't think of Graham cause he works in the computer department which has nothing to do with security. I should have at least realised that he could give me some phone numbers and names. Honestly, sometimes I wonder why I was born with a brain, seeing as how little I use it.

Anyway, I explain what's happened to Graham, and he says, no problem, he's willing to sort it out, but if he's going to do me a favour he wants one in return. Well, I'm thinking what could he want from me, apart from the obvious, and if he suggests that he's going to get a good slap in the face, in the middle of Malbury High Road. So I ask him what it is he wants, and he says he wants us to go out on a proper date. What's that mean, I ask, and he says with a proper meal and a film or go to a play or concert or something. You could have knocked me down with a feather.

Anyway, I think about it quickly, and if it's a proper date, and he doesn't try it on, well, where's the harm in that?

And I'm willing to do it cause it's for you, even if it's not you but the nasty one it's still sort of you if you see what I mean. So I told him, okay, but no funny stuff, and he says, of course not mademeselle (however you spell that), follow me.

So we go into the main office, he sorts out a visitor's pass for me at reception - they all know him and seem to think he's a great bloke, I was impressed. Then he takes me to where he works, sits down at his desk and starts typing something into his computer. Don't know what it was, but the next thing he's put an orange piece of paper into a printer, and out comes your security application as attached. Then off we go to the security department to get a signature. On the way I ask him how he did that seeing as we all know you can't reprint those things and he says he didn't reprint it cause we all know you can't reprint them. And I say I just saw him reprint it. And he says no I didn't I just saw him find it filed in the wrong in-tray where it had got lost.

And the penny drops and I say yes I did just see you find it in an in-tray where it had got lost, yes, of course, silly me, I forgot. Silly me? Graham doesn't even have an in-tray on his desk, the lying basket.

And we get to the security department where all the blokes there - overweight, you can see they eat too much, drink too much and smoke too much, but mostly a cheerful lot avoiding doing any work - anyway, they all know him and think he's a great guy as well. By now I'm wondering whether there's anyone he doesn't know who doesn't like him. Apart from the managers of course.

So he asks one of them to sign the form, and this bloke looks me over, says something like 'very nice', the way that sort do, though it wasn't like some of them do, you know, where you feel you need to have a shower afterwards. Anyway he says seeing as it's for him, Graham I mean, and since his girlfriend is such a stunner - meaning me - that's Graham's girlfriend, he'll do it but only for us.

Well, I did think of pointing out that I wasn't Graham's girlfriend, but by this stage my thoughts are all over the place, and you think it's one of those times just to let people think what they want to think, just so you get what you came for and leave it at that. So I got the signed application, told Graham, sorry, didn't have time for lunch cause I had to get back here cause there wasn't anyone else in the clinic (that was a little lie - not that there wasn't anyone else - there wasn't, and because there wasn't anyone else I didn't need to get back that quickly, no-one to tell me off for being away - but I knew he wouldn't notice) and raced back here to finish this off.

I don't know what to think now. I know I saw Graham print that application. But everyone knows you can't do that. And I think back to all those funny comments he made when we were talking about how you couldn't change the system. And all I can think is that he knows how to change it and he did put those funny comments in somehow, and he is guilty, if you see what I mean, only the word guilty doesn't sound right.

And the way he seemed to know everyone, and they all seemed to like him, well, it's like seeing him in a different light, if you see what I mean. Only I'm not sure if I see what I mean, if you see what I mean.

Anyway, that doesn't really matter. The main thing is, security application enclosed. All you have to do now is go down to the main office with a photograph, one of the small ones, and some ID like a passport. They'll do you a security card while you're there. I can't see you getting one before Monday, but don't worry I'll sort it out so that they don't know you haven't been looking after the window. But make sure you get it sorted for the next Monday, the 15th, because I am determined I am going to meet you, and when I get determined to do something I really get determined and it gets done. So do it.

Love

Sandi

xxxxx

Malbury Town Council

External E-Mail
Private And Confidential

From : Sir Henry Walters

To : Joseph Parker, General Secretary, Malbury Branch, GWAJAMWATU

Sent : 15:32:16 4th September 2003

Dear Mr Parker

Many thanks for your communication of 3rd September.

Unfortunately I was attending an anniversary lunch organised by the Council to remember the events of 3rd September 1939, and consequently missed your secretary. I have however had a chance to peruse the proposal you submitted, and apart from one or two minor details I believe the Council will approve my recommendation that we accept the proposal, on the strict understanding that the unfortunate situation was caused by over-zealousness on the part of employees who have since left the service of the Council. I must also insist that the names of those employees be kept confidential, as the situation was not really of their making, and your member should accept at least part of the blame. However, for practical reasons I will not insist on the latter part.

I look forward to our weekly meeting tomorrow afternoon. I am not sure whether Frank will be able to make the meeting, so perhaps you could bring your secretary along in case? If Frank is able to make it I am sure we could find something constructive for her to do.

Regards
Henry
Sir Henry Walters
Chairman
Malbury Town Council

To:The Administrator
Malbury Centre Health Clinic
43 Green Lanes
Malbury WS2 HH5

9th September 2003

Dear Sandi pp The Administrator

Thank you for your letter dated 4th September 2003.

You will be pleased to know that the issue has been successfully resolved with the aid of your extremely helpful, delightful, and I am so informed, very attractive colleague, who apparently has the same name as yourself. I must try to meet her to thank her in person.

Could you please send me a Claim For Expenses Form form?

Yours Faithfully

James Allbright

J Allbright
32 Pinetree Road
Malbury WS9 JG8

P.S.

My Dear And Sweet Miss Goodwin

I am not the nasty one, I am just as nice as the other nice one.

See you soon

Love

James

To: The Administrator
Malbury Centre Health Clinic
43 Green Lanes
Malbury WS2 HH5

9th September 2003

Dear Sandi pp The Administrator

Thank you for your letter dated 4th September 2003.

Enclosed please find the usual completed Claim For Expenses Form form in the standard sealed envelope.

Could you please send me another Claim For Expenses Form form?

Yours Faithfully

Jim Allbright

J Allbright
32 Pinetree Road
Malbury WS9 JG8

P.S.

Dear Sandi

A thousand thanks for sorting that out, I was beginning to think of booking into the local asylum until it was all over. I shall definitely have to buy you some flowers at least - do you have any preferences? I would buy Graham some flowers, but I think a date with you is more than enough reward for him, probably too much. To qualify for a date with yourself I reckon needs something like saving the world from destruction, possibly twice. In the same morning.

If Graham really was playing silly buggers with the computer system I think he'd better keep really quiet about it. If they find out it won't be an industrial tribunal he'll be going to, it'll be instant dismissal without the option. Much as I appreciate him printing that security application out, he's taking a hell of a chance. Tell him thanks very much, but not to do that sort of thing in future.

Kayley's got to go back to Australia in October. Her sister's getting married unexpectedly quickly - usual reason, though I thought shotgun weddings were out of fashion. I get the feeling that the unexpected situation wasn't that unexpected from her sister's side, and that her sister decided it was time to force the issue. Who knows? But now Kayley wants me to go with her. She said it will give me a chance to see Australia and decide if I like it. Her plan is that we go over for three months, make a long holiday of it, stay with her relatives to make it affordable. I wouldn't mind a holiday somewhere warm, now that the days are getter shorter and winter is on the way, but I can't say I've ever fancied Australia.

Kayley seems dead set on the idea for some strange reason. Why, I don't know, seeing as we've only being going out for a few months, and she's very much the independent sort. But I recognise all the signs from when my ex and I were still in love, and she wanted something. 'Darling' this, 'Sweetheart' that, much cuddling up and puppy dog eyes. I told her I'd think about it, and wonder of wonders, she didn't lose her temper. Just said 'Yes, darling' and gave me a kiss. If she thinks she can get around me that way she's mistaken. Anyway, I can hardly start a new job, never mind all the others, and then disappear for three months.

You'll be happy to know that I am now the new owner of a brand new Malbury Council security card, permitting said owner to wash one window of the Malbury Centre Health Clinic. I shall therefore be presenting myself at said clinic next Monday at oh-nine-hundred, washing of window purpose for. And, of course, finally meeting the beautiful Administrator within.

See you Monday

Love

Jim

GWAJAMWATU

General Workers Apprentices Journeymen Artisans Mens and Womens
Affiliated Trade Union

External E-Mail

Private And Confidential

From : Joseph Parker, General Secretary, Malbury Branch, GWAJAMWAT

To : Sir Henry Walters

Sent : 15:09:08 10th September 2003

Dear Sir Henry

Following on our negotiations in last week's meeting, I have discussed the
matter with the member concerned, and can confirm that the offer will be
accepted when formally proposed.

Yours Faithfully

Joe Parker

General Secretary, Malbury Branch, GWAJAMWAT

Delete the rest of this as per usual just to be on the safe side.

Not that it was easy. The Shafter smelt a rat, and wanted to wait while he
reread everything from A to flipping Z. Fortunately he couldn't find
anything, and finally agreed that we could accept. Good thing he's a lawyer
instead of a businessman, he might have held out for more. We really will
have to get rid of him.

See you on the course Friday.

Regards

Joe

Malbury Centre Health Clinic Senior Administrators' Department

43 Green Lanes, Malbury, WS2 HH5

To: J Allbright
32 Pinetree Road
Malbury WS9 JG8
Reference Code : ALLBRIGHTJAMES2003_0000000002

11th September 2003

1. Thank you for your letter concerning Glazing Maintenance Project, Reference KL/000001/AE/9/4.3. I have been informed by Malbury Council Ethics Oversight Department that, due to certain irregularities in the awarding of the contract, the contract awarded to your company must, under Council rules, be terminated.

2. The Council recognises that this is due to no fault of your own, and is prepared to offer compensation as agreed in the original contract. Should you wish to contest this payment you must contact Malbury Services Auditing Department. This Department is unable to enter into any correspondence with you over this matter.

3. As per your request I enclose Form ACC985, Claim For Expenses. You must return the form in the pre-paid envelope.

Yours Sincerely

S Goodwin

pp The Administrator

P.S.

To: Mr James Allbright

Nah, boo sucks. See, the baddie doesn't win all the time. Now Jim will have to get the contract.

Sandi

x

Malbury Centre Health Clinic

43 Green Lanes, Malbury, WS2 HH5

To: J Allbright

32 Pinetree Road

Malbury WS9 JG8

Reference Code : ALLBRIGHTJIM2003_0000000002

11th September 2003

1. Thank you for your letter concerning Glazing Maintenance Project, Reference KL/000001/AE/9/4.3.

2. The contract for this project has unexpectedly again become available. Since your bid was second on the final short-list, we are prepared to offer you the contract rather than reprocessing the tender. If you agree to accept, please return enclosed Forms TOC7623, Contract of Signature and Form SC8712, Application for Security Clearance (Local).

3. As per your request I enclose Form ACC985, Claim For Expenses. You must return the form in the pre-paid envelope.

Yours Sincerely

S Goodwin

pp The Administrator

P.S.

Jim!

Congratulations! You did it! Well, you and me together.
And if you're wondering what happened, well, me too.
Lucky there's a new woman at the main office, she
phoned me to explain about the termination of the
contract - normally they just send forms which don't tell
you anything. Anyway, it appears that they - just think of
'them' as 'they', cause I'm not sure who they are, and I
don't suppose it's important - had decided that there
was something fishy about the contract. She - the new
woman - had heard that it had been awarded for political
reasons - that's probably that thing the old cow put on
file about the National Front - and with the old cow
having suddenly left they presumed there had been a
little fiddling going on. They get very touchy about that
sort of thing, so rather than take a chance they decided
to pay off on the contract and restart the tender
process. I managed to persuade the new woman that that
would be a waste of money, since there were only two
tenders in the first place. Just as well she didn't check
too carefully, or she might have worked out they were
from the same person.

They're strange this lot. There's a lot of back-
scratching and underhand stuff going on, but every so
often they get all paranoid and start insisting on

something being totally above board. I'm not sure whether they don't mind a little bribery, but get the heebies if they smell politics, or if it's just the wrong day of the month or what. Still, who cares, I don't think a room full of shrinks could work them out.

I'll mail this right away, so it should arrive first thing tomorrow, and you'll have time to get your new security card in time for Monday. I've made sure the security form is there this time.

Sandi

xx

To: The Administrator
Malbury Centre Health Clinic
43 Green Lanes
Malbury WS2 HH5

14th September 2003

Dear Sandi pp The Administrator

Thank you for your letter dated 11th September 2003.

Naturally I was most concerned to hear about the termination of contract. As a voter and council tax payer I would be most interested to know the exact nature and extent of the 'irregularities' you mention; perhaps these should be highlighted in the media. As a businessman my prime concern is for my business and staff, and they are obviously upset at what appears to be a lack of confidence in them. I have promised them that the remuneration for the termination of contract will be shared equally. Hopefully the amount will be generous enough to prop up their sagging morale, and we can put the issue behind us. My lawyers advise me that this would be the best route, much as I feel it my duty as a citizen to ensure that any potential or alleged corruption in high places is revealed to the public.

Could you please send me a Claim For Expenses Form form?

Yours Faithfully

James Allbright

J Allbright
32 Pinetree Road
Malbury WS9 JG8

P.S.

To The Sweet And Sexy Miss Sandi Goodwin

I shall demand a recount! (Okay, maybe not.)

Love

James

To: The Administrator

Malbury Centre Health Clinic

43 Green Lanes

Malbury WS2 HH5

14th September 2003

Dear Sandi pp The Administrator

Thank you for your letter dated 11th September 2003.

Enclosed please find the completed forms ACC985, Claim For Expenses, and TOC7623, Contract of Signature in the standard sealed envelopes.

Could you please send me another Claim For Expenses Form form?

Yours Faithfully

Jim Allbright

J Allbright

32 Pinetree Road

Malbury WS9 JG8

P.S.

Dear Sandi

What are those people on? Have they escaped from a lunatic asylum somewhere? I was tempted to write to the Ethical Oversight bunch to complain - as the James bloke, not as me, I'm not going to argue against getting the job, that would look daft. Then again, it would probably look perfectly logical to that lot. To be honest, I don't think I have the stamina to get involved in that sort of thing. I quite like the sound of just being a humble window washer once again.

Amazingly I did get your letter first thing Friday morning, and hot-footed it around to get the security pass, but the contract wasn't in their computer system - apparently it only goes in when they receive the signed paper, so get those processes moving, and I'll be able to pick up the security pass later this week.

Kayley's still badgering me about going to Oz. I have to admit I'm well tempted to go for a couple of weeks, be good to have a decent holiday for a change, though I'd much prefer Majorca or somewhere like that. Have you ever been to Australia?

How did the date with Graham go?

See you Monday week (hopefully)

Love

Jim

Malbury Centre Health Clinic

43 Green Lanes, Malbury, WS2 HH5

To: J Allbright

32 Pinetree Road

Malbury WS9 JG8

Reference Code : ALLBRIGHTJAMES2003_0000000002

16th September 2003

To : J Allbright

1. Thank you for your letter concerning Glazing Maintenance Project, Reference KL/000001/AE/9/4.3.

2. I have passed your concerns on to the relevant department. You will be contacted by them shortly.

Yours Sincerely

S Goodwin

pp The Administrator

P.S.

To: Mr James Allbright, The Nasty Twin

You cheeky bugger! That almost looked like blackmail! Pay me enough and I won't go to the press. (Hope it works.)

Sandi

xx

Malbury Centre Health Clinic

43 Green Lanes, Malbury, WS2 HH5

To: J Allbright
32 Pinetree Road
Malbury WS9 JG8
Reference Code : ALLBRIGHTJIM2003_0000000002

16th September 2003

To : J Allbright

1. Thank you for your letter concerning Glazing Maintenance Project, Reference KL/000001/AE/9/4.3.

2. As per your request I enclose Form ACC985, Claim For Expenses. You must return the form in the pre-paid envelope.

S Goodwin

pp The Administrator

P.S.

Jim!

Have to be brief. I'm in a hurry to get your security application processed. Make sure you get your security pass before the weekend!

Hope to see you soon.

Sandi
xx

Internal E-Mail

From : P V Hamilton

To : Sir Henry Walters

Sent : 15:10:18 16th September 2003

Dear Sir Henry

More bad news I'm afraid. Just as we'd agreed to settle the mess with that obstreperous computer geek, up pops another problem. In brief: there's a little one-doctor clinic close to the main shopping centre which needed a window washed. Requests for tender for the job were published as per Council Rules, and the contract finally awarded. Unfortunately one of the junior staff apparently put on record that the awardee was a member of the National Front - put it on the computer record, would you believe. The Council Ethics Oversight Department got hold of it and blew their top. If it got into the public domain the media would have a field day. As you know, we can't change the computer data. We would have to go to the software suppliers, and you can only imagine what might happen then. Might as well broadcast the fact publicly ourselves.

We immediately decided to cancel the contract, as per Council Ethics Oversight Department advice, and offered it to the second on the shortlist. We offered full compensation to the original contractor as per the contract, hoping he would miss the fact that the contract did not have such a clause (and what idiot left that one out?). Unfortunately the contractor has written what is obviously a thinly disguised blackmail note - 'make it worth my while or I'll have a word with the press'. Hopefully he has not heard of the Data Protection Act, but even if he hasn't, any half-decent reporter will soon inform him, and then we will have to hand over all data, and if he isn't a member of the National Front we will be even deeper in you know what.

I think we will have to be very generous, make him an offer he can't refuse, and get him to sign a disclaimer at the same time. I'll get our lawyers on to it as soon as you give the go-ahead.

On second thoughts, I will get some private lawyers on to it. Ours do not appear to even understand the concept of terms of cancellation clauses.

I notice that all these problems have come to a head since Jane and Valerie left. I know we have had difficulty in replacing them with people of similar calibre, but it is obviously becoming a critical issue. As it is we are going to have to consider cutting costs somewhere immediately. I believe we will have to consider increasing the salary for Jane and Valerie's old positions to attract suitably qualified candidates. I know that that will breach the Grade Rules, and other staff will be unhappy if they find out, but there must be a way around it. We can't go on bouncing from crisis to crisis. It's even interfering with my golf.

Please let me know your views as soon as possible so that I can get the ball rolling. I will convene an emergency meeting of the Financial Expenditure Rules committee to identify areas suitable for cost cutting. Probably a library or two; it might get the press excited, but very few of the voters are bothered, and those who are did not vote the current Councillors in, I'm pretty sure of that. After all, that's what democracy's all about. As it will be an emergency meeting, Council Rules permit us to take action without recourse to Council agreement.

Which is one blessing at least.

Regards
Peter

To: The Administrator
Malbury Centre Health Clinic
43 Green Lanes
Malbury WS2 HH5

21st September 2003

Dear Sandi pp The Administrator

Thank you for your letter dated 16th September 2003.

And thank you for passing on my concerns to the relevant department. They have been most helpful in alleviating any worries I had, and I can only say that they have my fullest confidence. I suppose this will be my last correspondence with you, as the matter appears to have been settled.

Could you please send me a Claim For Expenses Form form? For old times' sake?

Yours Faithfully

James Allbright

J Allbright
32 Pinetree Road
Malbury WS9 JG8

P.S.

To: A Women Whose Efficiency Is Only Surpassed by Her Looks, Miss Administrator Sandi Goodwin

And very generous they were too. Offered more than I would have even thought of asking for. I'd better leave town before the council tax goes up to pay for it.

I think I'll give up writing as James. It was fun, but it's becoming too much like schizophrenia.

Love

James

To: The Administrator
Malbury Centre Health Clinic
43 Green Lanes
Malbury WS2 HH5

22nd September 2003

Dear Sandi pp The Administrator

Thank you for your letter dated 16th September 2003.

I duly obtained my security pass and presented myself at the clinic this morning, window washing for the purpose of. However I was prevented from thus doing by the security guards. They told me that the clinic was closed and thus my security pass invalid. Personally I fail to see the logic in that, but they appeared quite belligerent and unhappy, and I had fulfilled my part of the contract in attempting to wash the window. I cannot be held responsible for failing to do so because prevented by your overly large, and, may I say, rather aggressive, security staff. Could someone please explain what is going on?

Enclosed please find the completed Claim For Expenses form in the standard sealed envelope.

Could you please send me another Claim For Expenses Form form?

Yours Faithfully

Jim Allbright

J Allbright
32 Pinetree Road
Malbury, WS9 JG8

P.S.

Sandi, Sandi, Sandi

Do you ever have this urge to shoot yourself? Or a whole lot of other people?

I despair.

So what's happened now? The clinic was undoubtedly closed, no lights, even the goldfish tank looked switched off. I couldn't see clearly, but I could have sworn the fish were swimming belly-up on the surface. I don't know much about fish, but I think that normally means they're dead.

Looks like I'm off to Oz for a couple of weeks in October. Kayley found my one weak spot. She plied me with beer and managed to get me to say I did love her and I would go to Australia with her. She claims I agreed to three months, I can't exactly remember. I shall whittle it down to three weeks.

She knows some really low-down tricks, that one. She was wearing one of the flimsiest tops I have ever seen. What there was to see.

How are you and Graham doing?

How's Little Helen?

Love

Jim

43 Green Lanes, Malbury, WS2 HH5

To: J Allbright

32 Pinetree Road

Malbury WS9 JG8

Reference Code : ALLBRIGHTJAMES2003_0000000002

25th September 2003

To : J Allbright

1. Thank you for your letter concerning Glazing Maintenance Project, Reference KL/000001/AE/9/4.3.

2. As per your request I enclose Form ACC985, Claim For Expenses. For old-time's sake.

Yours Sincerely

S Goodwin

pp The Administrator

P.S.

To: mr James Allbright

Congratulations! Jammy bugger.

Sandi
x

Malbury Centre Health Clinic

43 Green Lanes, Malbury, WS2 HH5

To: J Allbright

32 Pinetree Road

Malbury WS9 JG8

Reference Code : ALLBRIGHTJIM2003_0000000002

25th September 2003

1. Thank you for your letter concerning Glazing Maintenance Project, Reference KL/000001/AE/9/4.3.

2. I have been informed by Malbury Council that, due to ongoing simplification of budgetary outlay and improvements in the service supplied by Malbury Council to residents, Malbury Centre Health Clinic has been closed down. This naturally means that the contract, Reference KL/000001/AE/9/4.3, must be terminated.

3. The Council recognises that this is due to no fault of your own, and is prepared to offer compensation as agreed in the original contract. Should you wish to contest this payment you must contact Malbury Services Auditing Department. This Department is unable to enter into any correspondence with you over this matter.

4. As per your request I enclose Form ACC985, Claim For Expenses. You must return the form in the pre-paid envelope.

S Goodwin

pp The Administrator

P.S.

Jim, oh, Jim where are you?

It never rains but it pours, or something like that. They
have closed the clinic because of 'low doctor-patient
ratio', meaning there weren't enough patients to keep it
open. Well, course there weren't, they made it bloody
nigh impossible for any patients to turn up. Poor sods had
to trek across town, or go to the hospital instead. I don't
want to even think about how many of the old codgers
simply gave up and stayed at home in misery. This lot
should be put in prison.

I've been transferred to head office for 'reassignment'.
The woman who did the cleaning at the clinic has been
told 'bye-bye' - she didn't have a proper contract, so she
didn't even get notice pay. Not that they gave any notice
to anyone. One day open, next day closed, e-mail on
Friday telling me to report to head office on Monday. Dr
Singh has been given early retirement. The security
guards are well pissed off cause they work for a
contractors, and with the clinic closed there's no work
for them once the council get rid of the lease, so the
contractor will let them go, no severance pay either.

The main reason I took the job at the clinic was that it
was close to my flat and Helen's kindergarten and new
school to be, so I could get her to school and pick her up
without much hassle. Head office is miles away, I had to

get Helen to kindergarten extra early on Monday and catch a bus to work, which means something else to pay for, and the salary isn't exactly a lot to start off with. Monday I worked out that I'd get a couple of pounds less if I was on the dole, but at least then I'd have time to look after Helen properly.

But I don't want to go on the dole! I don't want Helen to grow up thinking that it's normal. I don't want her little friends to think of her as the one with the Mummy who hasn't got a husband and can't get a job.

Sigh. I think Dad must have gone to the pub. He certainly hasn't been looking after me like he said. I wouldn't mind so much, but he could at least have done something for his granddaughter.

He would have loved Helen, you know.

Here I am again, feeling all sorry for myself. Sorry, I won't do it again, promise.

But it was a real bummer, Monday, I can't tell you how depressed I was. Didn't know any of the people I was suddenly working with, didn't know what I was supposed to be doing, didn't know whether I would have a job at all. Managed to struggle through the day, somehow, and I was leaving the office feeling like life just wasn't worth it, wondering whether I should turn up the next day, when I bump into Graham. Last I'd seen him was Thursday, he'd gone down to Brighton over the weekend to have a look at houses. He was only in the building to pick up his stuff, he's been given a payoff to leave his job with a good reference and everyone pretending they're terribly sorry to lose him, lucky bugger. Why does that sort of thing never happen to me?

Anyway, he asks why I'm looking so miserable, was it cause I hadn't seen him since Thursday, joking I think. He asks if I want a drink, and I really, really need someone to talk to, and I'm really fond of him anyway, so I say yes, just the one, and pour my heart out to him in the George. One drink becomes two, and it would have become a full bottle of gin if I didn't have little Helen to pick up. So he gives me a hug, which I really needed, tells me not to worry cause it will all be okay - what does he know, he doesn't have any problems - and gives me a lift to the kindergarten. Helen's all excited because uncle Graham is there, which sort of makes it worse, you know, she doesn't get excited cause Mummy's there, and Mummy really needed to feel wanted. So I tell Graham, thanks for the lift, we'll walk from here, and he says why don't we go out for dinner, the three of us.

Well, I don't feel like cooking anyway, and Helen does need something to eat, and she's all excited about the idea, so I say yes, okay, might as well. I've been on two proper dates with him already, I sort of agreed to another after the first one, and he's been really good company, so, why not? I desperately needed someone to talk to, Mum would be useless, and you weren't there. And he's really good with Helen, tells her she has to be extra-nice to Mummy cause Mummy's having problems at work, which I wasn't going to do cause I didn't want her worried, but she's a little darling, gives me a lovely hug and tells me not to worry cause she'll look after me. So I start blubbing like a little baby, and there's little Helen and Graham holding me and me feeling like a right idiot, but sort of enjoying it anyway, if you know what I mean.

Had a great meal at a restaurant which Graham said was 'child-friendly'. Apparently there aren't a lot of those. I wouldn't know cause I never have money to go to restaurants anyway. To start off I didn't feel like eating anything, but Graham orders a really nice wine and the food was scrumptious, so in the end I had loads, which made me feel even better. Helen wanted some wine of course, and I told her no, she was too young. After we'd got back to the flat and she was put to bed Graham and I had a cup of coffee, and he said maybe she could have had a little, little glass, like the French do, you know, their kids grow up knowing what alcohol is and how to handle it, our lot you have to wait until you're eighteen or whatever it is though we never did, and because it seems like such an adult thing to do they chuck it down their throats like there's no tomorrow - and my little Helen is NOT going to grow up that way.

The nice thing is that he waited until Helen was in bed to suggest it. Other people would have said it in the restaurant while Helen was there, and then of course you end up with arguments all the time, 'so-and-so says it's okay' and so on.

He promised to pick me and Helen up the next morning, drop Helen off, take me to work, since he wasn't doing much at the moment. I said, no bother, I'll get the bus, even though it would be a bother, but he said he's not taking no for an answer and he'd be there anyway, so there wasn't much I could do about that.

Anyway, Tuesday he's there as promised, we drop Helen at school, he drives me into work. It's like really depressing again, especially a meeting with one of the 'human resources' managers. Like you're just a resource to be used and dropped when you're no longer needed. And this manager effectively says there's no positions available anyway, but she'll find something for me to do in the meantime, only it won't be very interesting. As if what I was doing before was interesting! What she's saying is basically they're going to make my life as miserable as possible hoping I'll leave.

The only thing I had to look forward to was Graham picking me up after work. I told one of the girls that, and she said I was a lucky cow to have him for a boyfriend, all the girls fancied him. I said he wasn't my boyfriend, but she just laughed and asked what he was like in bed.

Horrible bitch. You can't imagine what it's like to work with people like that.

So Graham picks me up, then we collect Helen from school, back to my place for dinner, I figured I owed him that at least. I asked him what he'd been doing that day. After bending his ear about my day, though, which is a bit unfair on him. Anyway, he just laughs and tells me I'll find out the next day, but he's like that sometimes, says things which don't tell you anything.

So this morning he picks us up again, we drop Helen off at kindergarten, and we're driving in when he pulls over in a no-parking space. Then he gets down on one knee, pulls this box out with a diamond ring in, and asks me to marry him! Only it wasn't as easy as that cause he's trying to squash himself down between the seat and the steering wheel, his head's against the roof and then he's trying to get the ring out of his pocket, which is jammed against the seat, and I'm wondering if he's finally trying to do something perverted, only I couldn't imagine what. And it must have looked well dodgy from outside, cause he's just got the little box out when this copper opens his door and tells him we're under arrest for lewd acts in public. I think he thought I was some sort of prostitute. At eight o'clock in the morning!

So Graham says very pompously, 'Do you mind, officer, I am trying to propose to this young lady', and the officer says 'Yes, it's what you're proposing to do to her why I'm arresting you', And Graham says 'Don't be a fool, man, I am proposing marriage to her, what do you think I was proposing to do with an engagement ring?' And the copper's quite young, and you can see on his face he wasn't sure of what he thought, only he thought there was definitely some hanky-panky going on. So he looks at me suspiciously and asks, 'Is that correct Madam?' and I can only nod cause I'm shaking with laughter, tears running down my face, what with Graham trapped there having this strange conversation with a copper over his shoulder, and the copper bending over trying to see the ring. So the copper says, this is a no-parking zone anyway, and you aren't allowed to park here, and Graham says 'I am not parking here, I am proposing here, there aren't any no-proposing signs, and you are not making things any easier officer,' even more pompous like. So the copper says, sort of confused, 'Well, okay, sir, but move on as soon as you can', and he walks away quickly, like he didn't really want to know.

So Graham turns back to me and says, 'Miss Sandi Goodwin, will you do me the honour of being my wife,' and it's lucky I'm laughing so much cause I really don't know what to say, I mean like he's got a degree and everything and I'm only a single mum with hardly any O-levels, not the sort of woman he's likely to fancy. In the end he says 'I'll take that as a maybe', closes the box and puts it in my handbag, says 'have a think and let me know'. So we drive off to work and my brain is racing, I don't know what to say. It's all so unexpected, and I don't know, do I want to marry him? He's a great guy, loads of money, good looking, makes me laugh, he'd be a great father for Helen, so why am I not sure? And I really don't want to hurt him by saying no, he's too much of a friend. I think he's already hurt cause I'm sure he wanted to put the ring on my finger like they do in books, instead he had to put it into my handbag.

Please, please, please write soon and let me know what you think. I'll tell him after work I'll give him an answer in a week, only hope he doesn't say he wants a yes or no right away. I don't think he will though, he's not like that. And I'll tell him not to mention a word to Helen, cause if she finds out he's proposed and I haven't said yes she'll hate me forever.

What am I going to do????

Where are you when I need you most????

Sandi

xxxx

The Herald

26th September 2003

Comment

Reducing Services or Common Sense Budgetary Control?

This newspaper is well known for its criticism of the more foolhardy and nonsensical ideas Malbury Council is famous for coming up with. At the same time we will never indulge in the knee-jerk 'the capitalist barbarians are at the NHS door' reactions of some tabloids, either for political reasons or to sell more copies to a misled public.

It is true that the closure of Malbury Centre Health Clinic is only one in a long line of closures of public service facilities, along with libraries, schools and public toilets. it is also true that many of them were very popular and much needed and used, and the council deserves censure for a number of those closures. This time that is not the case, as anyone who has bothered to study the figures can see at a glance.

'A popular and central health care centre' bleat the left-wing journals. 'Another example of Labour mismanagement of the NHS', bleat the conservatives. Well, no, not quite. It may well be popular, as a general survey of local residents by this newspaper established, but it is only popular in that they rather like the idea. Figures provided by the council show that on average only five patients attend the clinic per week - one a day. There is no rational reason to continue to maintain such a low figure when better facilities exist only a bus ride away.

It may be central, but that is hardly a logical argument for keeping it open. In fact, it is an argument for closing it, since its very centrality means high rental rates, costing the taxpayer more, and denying the space to a business which could more profitably utilise the area and pay rates to the council for the privilege, thus reducing the taxpayers' burden. As for 'labour mismanagement of the NHS', the fact that the council are willing to take hard decisions at a time when we all need to tighten our belts shows proper management of resources.

No doubt these same people who condemn the council will foam at the mouth when tax rates have to go up to pay for the very under-utilised facilities they demand. They can't have it both ways. The decision to close the clinic is a welcome breath of fresh air. We look forward to seeing a new business open in its place, bright and full of promise, replacing the drab and unwashed exterior that, frankly, was a shameful disgrace and a complete waste of money.

To: The Administrator
Malbury Centre Health Clinic
43 Green Lanes
Malbury WS2 HH5

29th September 2003

Dear Sandi pp The Administrator

Thank you for your letter dated 25th September 2003.

While some might think there is a conflict of interests in this case, I cannot but wholeheartedly protest at the closure of yet another civic amenity. I feel so strongly I am thinking of joining the other citizens of Malbury in their protests outside the Council offices. However, as there is a potential conflict of interest, I am willing to consider the matter in the light of any explanation and remuneration you will be considering.

Enclosed please find the completed Claim For Expenses form in the standard sealed envelope.

Could you please send me another Claim For Expenses Form form?

Yours Faithfully

Jim Allbright

J Allbright
32 Pinetree Road
Malbury WS9 JG8

P.S.

Dearest Sandi

Well, probably won't work, but it's worth a try. I can hardly complain. I've never earned so much money for doing so little. But I might join the others in protesting against any council tax rise.

As far as Graham goes, I don't like to really say anything when I've never met the bloke, and, come to think of it, I've never actually met you, much to my great disappointment. But, since you have asked, I will give you my opinion. Remember, though, that you will be making the final decision, so you must do as your heart tells you.

Marry the poor sod! He's obviously in love with you, you know he's a computer geek, so I doubt if he spends his spare time robbing old ladies (though I'd keep an eye on him whenever he starts thinking of messing around with other people's computer systems). You're extremely fond of him, you said he was like a friend, and that's what makes great marriages - two people who are good friends. I'm not a psychologist, but I'd put ten quid on you being in love with him eventually. Make that a hundred quid. He sounds like a thoroughly decent bloke, a bit too romantic for modern times - how many blokes these days would propose before, well, you-know-what?

And if you want to look at the practical side, let's face it, how many blokes are you likely to meet that you like and Little Helen likes?

I reckon you're pretty jammy yourself. Wouldn't mind finding someone like that for myself. Well, not Graham of course, a woman who loves me like that, you know what I mean. I reckon your Dad finally came back from the pub in the sky.

Go ahead, say yes, you can always divorce him later if it turns out to be a mistake!

I haven't managed to convince Kayley that I only said three weeks in Oz, so I might be gone a little longer - I'll definitely send a postcard, at least one a week. At the moment I'm only going to have time to organise handing over my current jobs to other blokes, but I'm sure we could squeeze in time for a drink before I leave. The one we always planned on.

Say yes now!

Best of luck

Lots of love

Jim

Malbury Council Accounts Department

Malbury Council Centre, Park Road, Malbury, WS8 HT9

To: J Allbright

32 Pinetree Road

Malbury WS9 JG8

Reference Code : ALLBRIGHTJIM2003_0000000002

1st October 2003

1. Notification of payment

Details : Compensation for Termination of Contract and General expenses payment, breakdown attached

2. Payee : Jim Allbright

3. Account details : As specified in breakdown

4. Date of payment : 30/09/2003

5. Amount : £5,324.00 (Five thousand three hundred and twenty four punds and zero pence)

6. Accruals : £None (None)

7. Accrual Basis : Monthly interest

8. Method of Payment : Electronic Transfer

9. Contest : If you wish to contest this payment you must contact Malbury Services Auditing Department.

This Department is unable to enter into any correspondence with you over this matter.

10. Declaration : This payment has been automatically generated by our computer services. The amounts may not be muddified.

Malbury Council Accounts Department

Malbury Council Centre, Park Road, Malbury, WS8 HT9

To: J Allbright

32 Pinetree Road

Malbury WS9 JG8

Reference Code : ALLBRIGHTJAMES2003_0000000002

1st October 2003

1. Notification of payment

Details : Compensation for Termination of Contract and General expenses payment, breakdown attached

2. Payee : James Allbright

3. Account details : As specified in breakdown

4. Date of payment : 30/09/2003

5. Amount : £10,285.01 (Ten thousand two hundred and eighty five punds and one pence)

6. Accruals : £None (None)

7. Accrual Basis : Monthly interest

8. Method of Payment : Electronic Transfer

9. Contest : If you wish to contest this payment you must contact Malbury Services Auditing Department.

This Department is unable to enter into any correspondence with you over this matter.

10. Declaration : This payment has been automatically generated by our computer services. The amounts may not be muddified.

Malbury Centre Health Clinic

43 Green Lanes, Malbury, WS2 HH5

To: J Allbright
32 Pinetree Road
Malbury WS9 JG8
Reference Code : ALLBRIGHTJIM2003_0000000002

2nd October 2003

1. Thank you for your letter concerning Glazing Maintenance Project, Reference KL/000001/AE/9/4.3.

2. As per your request I enclose Form ACC985, Claim For Expenses. You must return the form in the pre-paid envelope.

S Goodwin

pp The Administrator

P.S.

Jim!

Had to do this in a hurry. Will write soon.

Sandi
xxxx

To: The Administrator
Malbury Centre Health Clinic
43 Green Lanes
Malbury WS2 HH5

5th October 2003

Dear Sandi pp The Administrator

Thank you for your letter dated 25th September 2003.

Enclosed please find the completed Claim For Expenses form in the standard sealed envelope.

Could you please send me another Claim For Expenses Form form?

Yours Faithfully

Jim Allbright

J Allbright
32 Pinetree Road
Malbury WS9 JG8

P.S.

Sandi

Well?

And?

Have you said yes?

Love (grudgingly given, I want the answer!)

(And I want the answer Yes!)

Jim

Malbury Centre Health Clinic

43 Green Lanes, Malbury, WS2 HH5

To: J Allbright
32 Pinetree Road
Malbury WS9 JG8
Reference Code : ALLBRIGHTJIM2003_0000000002

8th October 2003

1. Thank you for your letter concerning Glazing Maintenance Project, Reference KL/000001/AE/9/4.3.

2. As per your request I enclose Form ACC985, Claim For Expenses. You must return the form in the pre-paid envelope.

S Goodwin

pp The Administrator

P.S.

JIM! Darling, darling Jim!

Well, I had a word with my Mum about Graham, seeing as how I had nothing to lose, and she said much the same as you, except she called me a 'dozy little cow'. Really, from my own mother! Anyway, I decided that, what the hell, there was nothing to lose and everything to gain, and I really am very, very fond of Graham, though I wouldn't call it love, or not what I always thought love would be like.

So I decided that first I would tell little Helen. I was sure she would agree, but since she's got a stake in this it seemed unfair not to let her share the decision. When I told her she was ecstatic. Over the moon. I don't think I've ever seen her so pleased. And full of energy, it was almost impossible to get her to bed that evening. She was so excited about the thought of having a 'real' daddy, even more so because it was Graham. Said she was going to call him Daddy from now on, so I had to warn her not to do that, that she mustn't frighten him away, that it was his decision whether he wanted her to call him that. Poor little thing didn't understand why her calling him Daddy would frighten him away, but I've seen too many men run for cover once they find you've got a child, and then suddenly I didn't want anything, not the slightest thing, to make Graham think about changing his mind. I know he's really fond of Helen, but there's a huge difference between being 'Uncle' and being 'Daddy'.

We met Graham at the park early Saturday morning, we were going to go for a walk then have lunch and take in a movie in the afternoon. So we're waiting at the park gates when he walks up, and little Helen runs to him, jumps into his arms, and gives him ever such a big hug, looks in his eyes and says 'Hello, Daddy', the little minx! After all I'd told her! Anyway Graham didn't seemed to mind, he suddenly had this massive big grin on his face, like he'd won the lottery or something. And he puts Helen down, looks at me and says, 'I take it that means yes?' Well, I didn't say anything, just took the ring in its little box and handed it over to him.

His face was a picture. I've heard of the phrase 'jaw dropping on the ground', but I've never seen someone actually almost do that. He must have thought that I was saying 'No', by giving him the ring back like that. So I told him, 'I thought you'd like to put it on my finger, do it properly like', and suddenly there's this look of relief on his face, I thought he was going to cry. 'But if you even think about going down on one knee in public I'll wallop you' I warned him. I think he was so relieved he would have done anything I told him to. But he takes the ring out, takes my hand ever so gently, and puts the ring on my finger. Gorgeous it is, a real diamond, not brassy, but sort of classy, or stylish. Must have cost him a fortune.

So we had a great day, but the questions started popping up, the ones that do whenever you think life is perfect.

He mentioned meeting his mother, and I thought what will his mother think of me? Me a single mother with nothing, really, no education or career or anything marrying her son - maybe she would think I was a right little gold-digging tart. I thought his mother must be ever so posh, teacups in the drawing room and cucumber sandwiches with the edges cut off, that sort of thing. I suddenly realised how little I really knew about him, and I'd just agreed to marry him! What was I thinking about?

But I thought to myself, you're going to marry him, share your life with him, and like you said, marriage means being friends and trusting each other, talking to each other and trusting each other.

Funny, that, if you'd asked me whether I trusted Helen's father before he got found out, I wouldn't have been able to tell you. I thought I loved him, trust wasn't something that entered my mind. But I do trust Graham. I know that.

So I told him I was worried about meeting his mother, and cucumber sandwiches, and doing things properly. He just laughed and squeezed my hand. Turns out that his mother used to take in washing and do ironing to support him and give him a proper education, cause his Dad died when he was little, didn't have life insurance or whatever like my Dad, so they had to make do on the little she could earn. She didn't have an education either, and he reckons she wouldn't recognise a cucumber sandwich if you put up a big sign pointing to it saying 'cucumber sandwich'.

So we've got lots to learn about each other, but somehow I think it's going to be all right. I've agreed that we'll move down to Brighton, it'll be a pain for Helen losing her friends, but she didn't seem to mind, and anyway, I don't think she has many friends, bit like me I suppose. Graham insisted we had to choose a house together, seeing as we're all going to be living in it together. He said he'd seen a couple of nice places in Hove, and a really great offer in Bognor Regis, but I said there's no way I am going to have an address with Bognor Regis in it, and he just laughed and said okay.

I think he was winding me up, the sod.

So we're off to Brighton for a few days next week. We'll be staying with his Mum - she lives there, which I think is maybe why he wanted to move there anyway - and Helen and I will share a bedroom, and he'll be in his own one. 'Have to do this properly, MisS Goodwin,' he said to me. I feel like a trembling virgin bride, I must say. Strange, isn't it?

So everything's happening quite suddenly. The council are quite glad I'm leaving, I reckon. In a way I'm sorry to leave, but thinking about things, it was hardly a happy time. I think the other girls are very jealous of me. I have made a promise to myself to be a good wife to Graham. Not often people get a chance to be happy. Just wish my thoughts wouldn't whirl around like they are. Have to think about getting a wedding dress. A wedding dress! White and all, Graham insists. And Helen will be a bridesmaid. Most I ever dreamed of after Helen came along was a quick session in the registrar's office wearing something smart, then down the pub for a few drinks and a week in Marbella as honeymoon. Mum's even talking about my wedding trousseau! (Had to look that one up in the dictionary.)

You must come to the wedding. I insist. It will be in about six week's time. Graham says he wants to make sure we do get married, says he's afraid he'll lose me if he leaves it too long. Me, I'm going to keep a careful eye on him, he just might meet someone better than me, and there's enough of those around without kids.

I'll send an invitation as soon as I know the date, and where, and that sort of stuff.

Lots and Lots of Love

Sandi

xxxx

P.P.S.

I think you're right - Dad must have come back from the pub at last.

To: The Administrator

Malbury Centre Health Clinic

43 Green Lanes

Malbury WS2 HH5

12th October 2003

Dear Sandi pp The Administrator

Thank you for your letter dated 8th October 2003.

Enclosed please find the completed Claim For Expenses form in the standard sealed envelope.

Could you please send me another Claim For Expenses Form form? For old times' sake. I think I might frame it.

Yours Faithfully

Jim Allbright

J Allbright

32 Pinetree Road

Malbury WS9 JG8

P.S.

My Dearest Sandi

Congratulations! And pass my congratulations on to Graham. I'm sure you'll make a wonderful couple.

I'm afraid I won't be able to make the wedding - typical of our luck. Kayley and I fly out to Oz next week, so I'll be out there when you walk up the aisle. Kayley said something the other day about how people with a trade can earn a good living in Australia, and how I could learn a trade quite easily. Or I could join the police over there, with my experience. I think she's trying to tell me something.

I will send a postcard as soon as I get there. And I'll definitely be thinking of you on your wedding day. You must send photographs! I shall raise a toast in your honour. Unfortunately it appears that they only drink out of cans there, tinnies they call them, no pints. Kayley says I should drink wine instead of beer, it's better for me. Wine? I'd be a laughing stock.

Thinking of you always

Lots of Love and Good Luck

Jim

P.P.S

Give my regards to Graham. Tell him I think he's a lucky, lucky sod.
xxx

Malbury Council Senior Management

Internal E-Mail

From : P V Hamilton

To : All Staff

Sent : 11:09:12 14 October 2003

As you are all aware we have been searching for some time for senior staff to take up the positions left vacant by Valerie Grateley and Jane Thornton. Unfortunately, despite contracting professional employment agencies to concentrate on this requirement, we have not been able to attract suitable candidates. Consequently it was decided that we should contract out the requirement to a private firm, in line with current government thinking on public-private partnerships, as has been done with a number of projects, thus far highly successfully.

You will be glad to know that we have reached a decision after putting the contract out for tender, and we are very pleased to announce the signing of the contract with an extremely professional, dynamic and reputable company, the C-Girls. I am sure you will all strive to your utmost to help them in providing Malbury Council with the usual high standard of services.

On a lesser note, rumours have been passed around regarding pay increases. Discussions are underway with the unions concerned, and it is largely accepted that in these times we need to undergo a belt-tightening process. While we will do our utmost to ensure that everyone receives a fair deal, under the circumstances we must accept that we need to pursue a strict regime of cost-control.

P V hamilton

Senior Manger

The Herald

15th October 2003

Advertisement

Long Lease for Sale

Large business site lease available in prime business area. Frontage consists almost entirely of a glass window, ideal for forward-looking commercial sales. Available for immediate occupation. Contact Malbury Council Business Unit for further details.

Postscript

Sandi and Graham were married on the 1st of December 2004. They had a son a year later and christened him James Gavin.

After eight months working for a large insurance company Graham gave up computing and became a landscape designer. He formed his own company and bought a large second-hand truck. His business card also offers computer systems decommissioning services.

Helen divides her time between school, looking after her little brother and asking Mummy when she's going to have another baby.

Jim and Kayley settled down in a small town close to Sydney. Kayley gave birth to a girl whom they named Sue-Ellen Sandi.

Jim still insists that he is only in Australia for a holiday, but in the meantime has opened an English-style pub which is proving profitable.

The company C-Girls appears to have closed sometime during 2004.

The site that formerly housed the clinic is now a travel agents.

Jim and Sandi still communicate, sending each other postcards on a regular basis. They still plan to meet one day.

Other novels by Bill Dughaille:

The FFSG series (aka the Wellbury Chronics)

Summers

The first in the FFSG series.

Detective Sergeant Frank Summers is a man on a mission: to keep his head down, stay out of trouble and enjoy the relaxed atmosphere of the easy-going, genteel town of Wellbury, his new posting. It's a town just made for him, where, he believes, even the criminals take bank holidays off. But, while perceptive in his professional life, he tends to miss the subtleties in his private life. In this case he fails to realise that his own tranquillity is being threatened by three women and a philanderer. The fact that the women in question are his boss, his constable and the local pathologist adds just the touch of danger to his life that he had hoped to avoid. The philanderer has been dead several decades. The women are very much alive.

The Eighty-five-percenters

The second in the FFSG series.

Detective Sergeant Frank Summers is faced with an unexpected crisis as the staid citizens of the genteel town of Wellbury rapidly descend into disorganised anarchy after a sociology professor announces on radio that eighty-five percent of the population will die in a coming cull. The prediction appears to be coming true as apparently total strangers are felled one by one according to a list of the ten-most-disliked Wellburians, from nagging neighbours to estate agents ... and the police, at a poorly performing number ten. But Frank fails to realise that there is a graver danger closer to home. Three women have decided that he is their responsibility: his boss, his constable and the local pathologist have agreed to become best of enemies. Now they intend to re-arrange his fate the way it should be. And they aren't asking anyone's permission.

Fakes, Fraud and Deception

The third in the FFSG series.

Detective Sergeant Frank Summers is in the doghouse, despite having recently arrested an internationally sought con-artist. And since he is in the doghouse he has no intention of pointing out that there is something very strange about the attractive French police woman who has come to interview the arrested man, not to mention the two detectives claiming to be from Scotland Yard. Oh, no, he is going to stay well out of the way this time. Definitely.

Jokers

The fourth in the FFSG series.

The doctors have pronounced Detective Sergeant Frank Summers physically fit following recovery after his shooting, but his colleagues fear that his sense of humour was extracted along with the bullet. They are, as always, more than willing to interfere in his life in the pursuit of a good cause. If that wasn't enough, a bunch of criminals calling themselves the Joker Gang are laughing at him, the university students are creating mayhem during their rag week, and someone called The Shocker is trying to kill him. The only advantage is that it take his mind off of the ultimatum the three women in his life have given him, one that he has only until the Sunday to resolve. Or leave town.

Prophecies

The fifth in the FFSG series.

Detective Sergeant Summers is under a hex, otherwise known as his colleagues. First they don't want him to get married, then it is imperative it must happen. Then they decide that a prophecy has been made which threatens the wedding. They don't believe in prophecies, but aren't sure that prophecies understand that. So they'll have to Do Something About It. And if their bumbling efforts aren't enough to ensure he never makes it to the altar, he has to cope with visiting aliens and resident ghosts. He does have tiny Squishy to protect him, but what match can even this plucky little kitten be against a prospective mother-in-law?

Loonymoon

The sixth in the FFSG series.

The Inspectors Summers have tied the knot and embarked on their honeymoon in a small family-run hotel in Normandy. She has very definite ideas of what she wants out of a honeymoon: to set a seal on their love, and to form a foundation for life-long devotion. He just wants to nick a French police officer's kepi. He had a Bobby's helmet nicked from him once by a French girl while he was on crowd duty one New Year's Eve in London, and now he intends to return the favour. Neither is about to achieve their aim unless they can solve the mystery of the woman in the bath and the missing heroin. Which means pitting their minds against the French Inspectors Simenon. That's Mr and Mrs Simenon, whose marriage has gone beyond the rocks and is now beating itself to death against humdrum reality. One or either or both or neither could be the guilty crumpet. More importantly, is their marriage a portent of what could become of the Loonymooners? Ultimately the decisive question could well be: which side do the peas go?

Others:

Diary of a Sane Man

In a cross between 'Last Of The Summer Wine' and 'One Flew Over The Cuckoo's Nest', set against a backdrop of the brave new world of New Labour's end of honeymoon, Fred is the Last Cynical Optimistic Realist.

Believing that he's found the perfect niche – three square meals a day plus all the newspapers he can read just for occasionally pretending to be mad – he's not going to be the one to rock the apple cart. Oh, no.

Safe from the wiles of women and the woes of the world, he's not going to rock the boat. Oh, no.

No, he's just going to sit and observe, and comment quietly on the insanity of life outside.

Well, maybe just little one tug of the loose strand of wool on life's jersey ...

Did you know they elected a monkey as mayor in Hartlepool?

The Weekend At Longwood

A whodunnit in the classic sense, set against the backdrop of World War II and the trials, tribulations and romances of nine suspects.

A group of friends get together during the last weekend of August 1939 at the rural retreat named Longwood, just a few miles from Portsmouth. They are there to celebrate the last time they will see Georgina Riley, famed American novelist and socialite, for some time, as she is scheduled to leave for her native New York in order to marry her childhood sweetheart. During the afternoon they good-humouredly assign to each other the most suitable names of the nine muses, the daughters of Zeus and Mnemosyne:

Calliope: the muse of epic poetry and rhetoric

Clio: history

Erato: love poems and mimicry

Euterpe: lyric poetry

Melpomene: tragedy

Polymnia: hymns to the gods and heroes

Terpsichore: dance

Thalia: comedy

Urania: astronomy, astrology and prophecy

The following morning Georgina is discovered in her bedroom covered in blood, her throat slit, barely alive. Her American maid is dead. A tiara Georgina had been flaunting the day before has disappeared.

Detective Inspector Rudman arrives to investigate. But with Georgina in a coma and no solid evidence there is little he can do apart from haunt their lives. With Germany's invasion of Poland a week later they disperse across the land, some to the air-force, some to the army, others to reserved civilian jobs.

But Rudman does not give up. Wherever they are he can be found. Whatever other duties he is tasked to, he will find time to keep tabs on them. Whatever the defeats and victories of the Allied cause, he has only one aim: to find the person responsible for the murder done that weekend in Longwood.

The war ends; some of the Muses have survived, some not. Some have prospered, some married, some matured, others have found despair. And then comes invitation to spend another weekend at Longwood. The message is that Rudman has found the evidence he has been looking for.

And so one of the surviving couples motor slowly down to Portsmouth, remembering the original weekend, the trials and the tribulations of the past years, and wonder: what will be revealed during the coming weekend at Longwood?

Firelight

A modern-day tale of an ordinary family gathering at Christmas; the good, the bad, the dysfunctional and the forgotten.

George Browne and his wife Winifred have retired to a large, run-down pile in the country. Rumour has it that it was once the abode of a mad aristocratic family with a penchant for Satanism, and that both they and their victims still haunt the corridors. Other rumours are that it was a lunatic asylum for much of the nineteenth and twentieth century, and bodies of the inhabitants are buried around the large gardens in unmarked graves.

The Brownes are an unremarkable retired couple who, depending on who you might ask, have bought it as an investment, or alternatively as somewhere with enough bedrooms to accommodate their children, grandchildren, and the little baby great-grandchildren. Too often in the past excuses have been made at special times, the most common of which has been of the "I don't want to put you to any trouble" variety. That excuse can no longer hold water.

Now it is approaching Christmas. Winter has set in, but the house is snug with oil heaters and real fires. As the various relations arrive, or don't arrive, it becomes clearer why invitations might have been refused in the past. The men of the family believe in having their way. The women of the family are strong-willed in their own different ways, and have various means of getting what they want.

The guests of the family - friends, boyfriends, girlfriends, wives and husbands - discover that their partners have a totally different side to them as the explosive hatreds of long-nurtured fights and feuds simmer to the surface before quickly boiling over.

One evening Winifred Browne encourages them to each tell a story as they sit in the lounge with the large fire warming them, the television off, no access to broadband, computers or mobile connections. Reluctantly at first they begin. As each evening passes: with different members taking turns, they announce in stories the feelings and hopes they cannot voice in public.

Finally it's the turn of Winifred Browne. Her story will be the one that tells them who they are, where they come from, and maybe why they have turned out the way they have.

For further details on these visit:
www.dughaille.info

www.ingramcontent.com/pod-product-compliance
Lightning Source LLC
Chambersburg PA
CBHW070833250626
47159CB00003B/762